"HE'S A LAWMAN, A U.S. DEPUTY MARSHAL."

Longarm was still hunkered down by the fire. Wallace was only a few feet away, staring at him with a mixture of disbelief, suspicion, and anger.

"Well?" Wallace said harshly. "What about it, Parker?"

"His name isn't Parker," Nora said before Longarm could say anything. "It's Long, Custis Long."

"Long," Wallace said, and then his eyes widened in shock as a realization hit him. "Son of a bitch, you're the one they call Longarm!"

For an instant, Longarm thought about trying to talk his way out of this, but then he realized he wasn't going to be able to do that. Wallace was already reaching for his gun. So Longarm did the only thing he could do.

He threw the potful of scalding coffee right in Wallace's face . . .

TABOR EVANS

LONGARM

AND THE
VANISHING VIRGIN

J
JOVE BOOKS, NEW YORK

LONGARM AND THE VANISHING VIRGIN

A Jove Book / published by arrangement with
the author

PRINTING HISTORY
Jove edition / May 1999

The Penguin Putnam Inc. World Wide Web site address is
http://www.penguinputnam.com

ISBN: 0-515-12511-3

A JOVE BOOK®
Jove Books are published by The Berkley Publishing Group,
a division of Penguin Putnam Inc.,
375 Hudson Street, New York, New York 10014.
JOVE and the "J" design
are trademarks belonging to Penguin Putnam Inc.

PRINTED IN THE UNITED STATES OF AMERICA

10   9   8   7   6   5   4   3   2   1

LONGARM

AND THE
VANISHING VIRGIN

Chapter 1

Longarm said, "Just put that gun down, old son. There's no need for anybody to die here."

The Dragoon Colt trembled slightly in the hand of the kid pointing it at Longarm. From where Longarm stood, the muzzle of the ancient percussion revolver looked about as big around as the mouth of a cannon. Longarm wondered if the kid was shaking because he was nervous, or because that blasted Dragoon was so damned heavy. Either way it was worrisome.

The kid lifted his other hand and wiped the back of it across his mouth and the wispy mustache on his upper lip. The mustache was likely part of an effort to look older than he really was, which was about sixteen, thought Longarm.

"I know why you're here," said the kid. "You're after me."

"Fella, I never even knew you existed until I walked into this saloon a few minutes ago," Longarm assured him. "And if you'll put that gun away, I might just disremember you pulling it on me. Maybe. If you'll put it up right now."

The kid shook his head. "Hell, no. You think I'm goin' to trust the word of a *lawman*?" He packed all the contempt in the world into the word.

Longarm sighed and glanced around the room. Nobody

showed any signs of wanting to pitch in and lend him a hand. He supposed he couldn't blame them. After all, he was a stranger in this little town, and a star packer to boot. Could be there were other men in this saloon besides the kid who wouldn't mind seeing him dead.

"You're right about one thing: I'm a United States deputy marshal. But I swear, I'm not after you, kid. Whatever you did that you think has got me on your trail, you're wrong."

The kid snorted in disbelief. "You're the one they call Longarm, ain't you?"

"Some do," admitted Longarm.

"I've heard about you. You don't never stop once you go after a man. And you don't bring in many prisoners alive and kickin' neither. If I put my gun up, you'll wind up shootin' me in the back and claimin' I tried to get away from you."

Longarm's jaw tightened in anger. One of the bad things about having a reputation of sorts was that folks didn't seem to mind embellishing on it any time the notion struck them. He'd never shot a helpless prisoner in the back. Never would. But he'd play hob convincing this addlepated youngster of that.

The bartender, a tall, thick-bodied man with graying hair and a craggy face, put his hands on the bar and leaned forward a little. "Why don't you light a shuck out of town, kid?" he suggested. "We'll keep this law dog here for a while, give you a start. No need for any shooting."

Clearly, he didn't want any blood getting on the floor. Longarm could understand that. Bloodstains were hell to get out of wood.

"I don't know," the kid said. "He'll just come after me later. He knows about that bank I robbed up in Kansas."

The bartender sighed. "Well, now he does anyway."

"Was it a federally chartered bank or a state-chartered one?" asked Longarm.

"Huh?" said the kid.

"If it was a state-chartered bank, then robbing it was a

2

state crime," Longarm explained patiently. "I'm a federal lawman. A state crime would be out of my jurisdiction."

The kid frowned in concentration as he tried to puzzle out what Longarm had just said. Finally, he nodded. "Yeah, it was a state bank. Leastways, that was the name of it. First State Bank of Hugoton."

Longarm had been keeping his hands in plain sight, just so the kid wouldn't get more nervous than he already was. Now he spread the fingers a little and said, "Well, there you go. I got no cause to arrest you. Just don't go back to Kansas."

"See," said the bartender, "no need for any shooting. I was right."

The barrel of the old Dragoon Colt started to dip toward the saloon's sawdust-littered floor. "Yeah, I reckon. . . ." the kid began. Then suddenly, his face twisted, and he jerked the gun up again. "I reckon I'll kill you just to make sure, lawman!"

The young would-be desperado talked too much, a common problem among those his age who wanted to make a name for themselves. By the time the last word was out of his mouth, Longarm had already thrown himself into a rolling dive that carried him behind an empty table. The kid jabbed the gun in his direction and pulled the trigger. Noise and flame and smoke geysered from the barrel of the Dragoon. The heavy lead ball it fired slammed into the top of the table, chewing up a long, ragged splinter.

Longarm palmed his own Colt from the cross-draw rig at his waist and fired twice over the table. The first bullet hit the kid halfway between his belly button and the hollow of his throat, and as he bent over a little in response to the hammer blow of the slug, the second shot tore through his heart. That one drove him back against the bar. He bounced off and fell facedown on the floor. He didn't move after he landed.

"Son of a bitch!" Longarm said fervently.

He hadn't wanted to kill the kid. He had meant every word

he'd said about letting the boy put the gun away and move on. But once the shooting started, Longarm's instincts had taken over. Well-trained nerves and muscles had drawn and aimed and fired the two shots, either of which would have been fatal. That was a legacy of the years Longarm had spent as a deputy marshal, years full of armed confrontations in which he'd had no choice but to kill or be killed.

With the smoking Colt still in his hand, Longarm looked around the room. The saloon was long and narrow, ugly on the outside with unpainted walls and a tin roof, and it wasn't much prettier inside. The customers consisted of half-a-dozen cowboys, a couple of men who were probably buffalo hunters who didn't know or didn't care that most of the buffalo were gone, and a pasty-faced gambler in a stained and threadbare frock coat. The bartender probably owned the place too, and the only other person in sight was a soiled dove with a pale, heavily painted face and a flabby body in a too-tight spangled dress. None of them seemed overly concerned about the dead young man lying bleeding on the floor.

"I told him to ride on," the bartender said with a sigh.

"That you did," agreed Longarm. He gestured at the body with the gun in his hand. "There going to be any trouble about this?"

"Who from? There's no sheriff hereabouts. I'd say you're the only law within fifty miles, mister. And the kid didn't have any friends or relatives around here either. He just drifted in a couple of days ago, spent all his time either drinking or poking Maggie over there. He seemed to have plenty of money to spend, so I wasn't in any hurry to run him off."

Longarm nodded, satisfied with the barkeep's answer. He raised his voice a little and asked, "Anybody know the kid's name?"

"He called himself Billy," offered the whore. "That's all I know."

Billy, thought Longarm. Probably wasn't his real name. Likely he'd taken it because of that other Billy who was famous here in New Mexico Territory, the one who helped raise hell and shove a chunk under the corner over in Lincoln County. He'd become a hero to every youngster with a gun and a dream of being a big man.

Longarm holstered his Colt. "You can carve that on his marker," he said, "or just leave it blank if you want."

"That's assuming that somebody'll pay for the burying," the bartender pointed out.

Longarm dug in his pocket and brought out a gold piece. He dropped it on the bar disgustedly. "There. That ought to cover it." He'd turn in an expense voucher for the money when he got back to Denver, and if Billy Vail didn't want to approve it, Longarm supposed he could cover the debt himself. He'd killed the kid, after all.

The bartender scooped up the coin and said, "That's enough, I reckon, with some left over for a drink. What'll you have?"

"I suppose it's too much to hope you've got some Maryland rye back there."

The bartender shook his head. "We're plumb out. Bar whiskey or beer, that's all."

The beer was probably watered down within an inch of its life, and the bar whiskey was likely brewed up in a galvanized washtub out back. But since those were his choices, Longarm said, "Whiskey," and hoped the stuff wouldn't give him the blind staggers.

The bartender poured the whiskey from a bottle with a peeling label into a glass that only had about a dozen fingerprints on it. He pushed the glass across the bar to Longarm and asked, "What brings you to Ashcroft?"

"Looking for something," said Longarm. He tasted the whiskey and tried not to make a face.

"And what would that be, that you're looking for, I mean?"

Longarm set the glass down, looked across the bar at the man, and said, "A bride."

Chapter 2

As he had climbed up the steps to enter the Federal Building in Denver a few days earlier, Longarm had been in a sour mood despite the beautiful June morning. The widow woman with whom he regularly kept company had chased him off for a spell. She'd gotten her back up because he had forgotten the anniversary of the first time they'd ever gone to bed together. Longarm couldn't quite understand what was so bad about that. To him, the *next* time was more important than the *first* time.

He paused just outside the pillared entrance of the building to light a cheroot and reflect on the matter. It wasn't like she was the only woman in Denver who would welcome him into her bed. There was a lady faro dealer in one of the saloons who was fond of him, not to mention that gal at the public library who'd let her hair down and taken her spectacles off a few times with him. It'd serve that widow woman right if he just went and found somebody else.

None of which thoughts improved his mood any, for some reason. He drew deep on the cheroot, and blew out a cloud of smoke.

What he really needed was something to do. It wasn't good for a man to sit around and brood over his personal dilemmas all the time. He'd been stuck here in Denver for nearly a month, and in that whole time, not one person had taken a shot at him or tried to stab him or trample him under the hooves of a horse. No wonder his nature had turned foul. He was bored.

Maybe this was the day Billy Vail would have something for him to do.

"Mornin', Henry." Longarm tried to make himself sound cheerful as he came into the outer office of the chief marshal and greeted the pasty-faced clerk who played the typewriter. He added hopefully, "I reckon Billy wants to see me."

"As a matter of fact, he does," said Henry. "He told me to send you right in whenever you got here." Henry frowned a little. "That was over half an hour ago."

Longarm bit down on the smoldering cheroot to keep from snapping back at Henry. You couldn't blame a fella for coming in late some mornings when he hadn't had anything to do for so long.

The big lawman's long strides carried him across the outer office to Vail's door. He opened it without knocking and stepped into the chief marshal's inner sanctum. "Howdy, Billy," Longarm said. "I hear you want to see me."

Vail's desk was cluttered with papers, as usual. Without looking up from shuffling them around, he waved a hand at the red leather chair in front of the desk and said, "Sit down, Custis. Be with you in just a minute."

Something about his voice told Longarm that Vail's casual pose was just that—a pose. Billy had a burr under his saddle.

After a moment, Vail shoved some of the papers aside and glanced at the banjo clock on the wall. "Well, I had hoped to tell you a little about this case before our visitors got here," he said peevishly, "but there's no time for that now. They'll be arriving any minute."

Longarm frowned. "Company coming, Billy?"

"Important company. I want you to mind your manners, Custis."

"Hell, I'm always polite—"

The door opened before Longarm could finish his sentence. Henry stuck his head in and said in a loud whisper, "They're here, Marshal Vail."

Vail stood up and motioned for Longarm to do the same. "Show them in," he said to Henry.

Henry retreated, then reappeared quickly, leading two men. Both of them wore expensive suits, boiled shirts, and silk ties fastened down with gem-encrusted tie clasps. The main difference in them was their ages: one was in his late thirties, the other probably twenty years older.

"Gentlemen, good to see you again," Vail said heartily. "Come in, come in. Have a seat." He waved Longarm over to one of the other chairs, leaving the one directly in front of the desk vacant for the older of the two visitors.

Longarm recognized both of them, and only his years of experience at not immediately revealing his emotions kept the surprise off his face. He wondered what a United States senator and one of the wealthiest railroad barons in the country wanted with a couple of civil servants like him and Billy Vail.

The older man, whose name was Bryce Canady, sat down in the red leather chair and folded his hands on the silver head of the walking stick he carried. He had a shock of crisp white hair, and his weatherbeaten features showed that he hadn't spent his entire life in an office, not by a long shot. In fact, he had started out swinging a sledgehammer on a crew building a railroad in Virginia more than thirty years earlier, if Longarm recalled correctly the newspaper articles he had read about the man. From there he had worked his way up to a position of riches and power as one of the top men in the cartel that controlled many of America's railroads.

The other man was one of the youngest to ever be elected to the United States Senate. Jonas Palmer was strikingly handsome, with dark hair and muttonchop whiskers framing a face that had the hearts of Denver's single women—and their mothers—fluttering to beat the band. But Palmer was no longer one of the most eligible bachelors west of the Mississippi, Longarm recalled. He was either about to be married, or perhaps already was. Longarm wasn't sure which because he didn't keep up that well with society goings-on. But he remembered the name of the young woman that Senator Palmer was going to marry.

Nora Canady. The daughter of the man sitting here in Billy Vail's office.

What in blue blazes was going on?

"Thank you for seeing us on such short notice, Marshal," Bryce Canady said in a deep, slightly hoarse voice.

These days, since he was riding a desk instead of a horse, Vail frequently had to be as much a politician as he was a lawman. He nodded solemnly and said, "We could have come to your house, Mr. Canady—"

The railroad baron waved a hand. "No, when I have business with a man, I like to come to his place of business. Just a habit of mine, I suppose, but it's stood me in good stead all these years. I like to see a man in his usual surroundings. That lets me size him up better." Canady glanced over at Longarm. "And this, I suppose, is the man you spoke of yesterday."

"Deputy Marshal Custis Long," Vail said. "Custis, this is Mr. Bryce Canady and Senator Jonas Palmer."

Longarm restrained the impulse to tell Vail that he knew who the visitors were. Instead he leaned forward in his chair and shook hands with Canady, then stood and stepped over to shake with Palmer as well. Both men had good, firm clasps. In orator's tones, Palmer said, "I'm pleased to meet you, Marshal."

"We've heard a great deal about you, Marshal Long," Canady said as Longarm resumed his seat. "Enough so that Jonas and I are convinced that you're the man to handle a rather delicate task for us."

Longarm glanced at Billy Vail, who wore a rather uncomfortable expression now. Vail didn't give Longarm any indication of how he was supposed to proceed, though, so Longarm bulled ahead on his own.

"Begging your pardon, Mr. Canady, but just so you ain't

laboring under the wrong impression, I work for the federal government. I don't handle any private errands for folks.''

''We understand that you're a law enforcement officer, Marshal Long,'' said Palmer, ''but if you'd just hear us out . . .''

''We need your help, Marshal,'' said Canady. ''It's sometimes not easy for a man such as myself to admit that he needs help from anyone, but in this case . . . Well, let's just say these are special circumstances.''

''All right, let's say that. What sort of circumstances are we talking about?''

''My daughter is gone.'' There was genuine pain in Bryce Canady's voice as he spoke.

''The woman I was about to make my wife,'' added Palmer, sounding just as upset as Canady.

''Gone,'' Longarm repeated.

''Disappeared,'' said Billy Vail. He held out a piece of paper toward Longarm. ''I wrote this report myself, Custis. It's not to leave this office.''

Longarm took the document, and quickly scanned the words written on it in Vail's blunt scrawl. After a moment, not even his studied stoicism could keep him from glancing up at Canady and Palmer. ''Miss Nora vanished on the night before her wedding?''

Palmer nodded as though it hurt him to admit it. ''On the very eve of our nuptials,'' he said.

''Could she have been kidnapped?'' asked Longarm, thinking like the lawman he was.

Canady shook his head. ''That possibility occurred to us as well, Marshal, but it's very doubtful. As you may know, I'm rather a wealthy man.''

''I'd heard,'' Longarm said dryly, ignoring the warning look that Billy Vail shot at him. ''That's why I brought up kidnapping.''

''Well, of course I take precautions, especially where my home and family are concerned. No one could simply waltz into my house and kidnap Nora. There were guards on duty outside, and servants inside.''

"But she still disappeared," Longarm pointed out. "If she left on her own, wouldn't the servants and the guards have seen her?"

"Perhaps . . . but you have to remember, Marshal, Nora grew up in that house, on that estate. She might well know ways in and out that no one else does. You know how children like to explore.''

"Not firsthand, but I reckon I know what you mean.'' Longarm rattled the piece of paper in his hand. "This says some of her things were missing.''

Canady nodded. "A carpetbag and a few of her clothes. And a pair of small, framed photographs. One of her mother and one of, ah, me.'' The railroad baron cleared his throat and looked a little embarrassed. He was probably a lot more accustomed to dealing with numbers than he was with emotions, thought Longarm.

"Is that all she took with her?''

"One other thing,'' said Canady.

Longarm waited.

"She took a gun,'' Canady finally said. "A small pistol. At least, I assume she took it. It's missing from my desk, but I didn't notice that until a couple of days after Nora had disappeared. I feel certain that she took it with her for protection.''

"Protection from what?''

"Well . . . whatever she might encounter, wherever she might have gone.''

For a tycoon, Canady was a vague son of a bitch, mused Longarm. But as he had thought a moment earlier, this was probably unfamiliar territory for a man such as Canady.

"Can she shoot a gun?'' Longarm asked.

The question brought an emphatic nod from Canady. "Yes, she can. I saw to it that she knows how to handle a weapon.''

"She's an excellent shot," added Palmer. "We've gone hunting together before."

That was a nice romantic thing to do for a couple of folks who were engaged, thought Longarm. He kept that comment to himself and said instead, "There was no note or anything like that left behind?"

Canady shook his head. "Nothing. She was just . . . gone."

"And this was . . . ?"

"Three days ago. The wedding was supposed to be on Sunday afternoon, and the last time anyone saw Nora was on Saturday night."

Longarm nodded. This situation was mighty puzzling, all right—why would a gal run away from home when she was about to get married to a handsome, influential gent like Jonas Palmer?—but Longarm still didn't see that it had anything to do with him.

"I'm mighty sorry about everything that's happened," he said, "but it seems to me that this is a matter for the Denver police."

Canady and Palmer were both shaking their heads before the words were finished coming from Longarm's mouth. "We can't risk going to the police," Palmer said. "It's vitally important that the newspapers not get wind of what's happened."

"I'm sure the police would mean to be discreet," added Canady, "but there's simply too much chance that the news could get out."

Longarm had to think about what that meant, but only for a moment. Like all politicians, Palmer was loved by some of the papers and hated by others. As a railroad baron, the same was true of Bryce Canady. If it became common knowledge that Canady's daughter had run away from home rather than marry Palmer, some of the papers would play up the story for all it was worth—and more—just to hurt Canady's business and damage Palmer's political career. The two men might be genuinely concerned about Nora's welfare, but at the same time, they were pragmatic enough to worry about how the story would look in the papers.

Longarm mentally pawed through those ruminations for a minute, then said, "I recall seeing stories in the papers about how the wedding was coming up. How did you explain that it didn't happen when it was supposed to?"

"We've told the press that the wedding was postponed due to an unexpected illness," Canady said.

"You told the reporters Miss Nora was sick?"

"No. We said that my wife was ill." Canady's fingers tightened on the head of the walking stick again. "As a point of fact, that happens to be true. My wife is so distraught over Nora's disappearance that she has taken to her bed."

Longarm tossed the report Billy Vail had written onto the chief marshal's desk, then leaned back in his chair and cocked his right ankle on his left knee. He wanted another cheroot, but he wasn't sure how Billy would feel about him lighting up right now.

"So Miss Nora's gone, the papers don't know it, the police don't know it, and you want me to find her," he said.

Both visitors nodded. "Can you help us, Marshal Long?" asked Palmer.

Longarm looked across the desk at Vail. "What do you think, Billy?"

Vail shrugged his shoulders and said, "I reckon I can't help you on this one, Custis. It's up to you. I can't order you to take an assignment that's technically out of our jurisdiction."

The answer didn't particularly surprise Longarm, and he knew Vail meant it. Billy was just as human as the next fella, and when a couple of gents as rich and powerful as Bryce Canady and Senator Jonas Palmer came to him asking for his assistance, his first impulse would be to help them. But Billy Vail was a lawman, first and foremost, and he wasn't going to force anybody else to bend the rules, not even for a good cause. Longarm knew that he could turn down this job if that was what he wanted.

On the other hand, he sort of felt sorry for Canady and Palmer. He was curious too about a gal who would take off for the tall and uncut less than twenty-four hours before she was supposed to marry the most eligible bachelor in the state. Longarm shifted in his chair, tugged on his earlobe a couple of times, frowned in thought, and finally cleared his throat before saying, "I reckon I could look into it a mite, see what I can turn up."

Bryce Canady's rugged face split in a grateful grin. "Thank you, Marshal," he said as he stuck out his hand. "I can't tell you how much we appreciate this. I'm sure you'll be able to find Nora. Marshal Vail says that you're the best man on his staff."

"He does, does he?" asked Longarm as he shook hands with Canady. He shot a sly grin at the uncomfortable-looking Vail.

Palmer shook hands again with Longarm too, and said, "You'll keep us apprised of your progress, won't you, Marshal?"

"If I find out anything, I'll let you know as soon as I can." Longarm looked at Canady. "I'll have to come to your house and poke around a little."

Canady frowned. "Is that absolutely necessary?"

"Might be something in Miss Nora's room that'd put us on the right trail," Longarm said. "I reckon you've probably searched it already, but sometimes a fresh set of eyes sees something everybody else missed."

"Very well. Can you come this evening? After dark?"

Longarm shrugged. "Sure, if that's what you want."

"I think it might be best. Less chance of someone from the newspapers seeing you that way."

"Won't the reporters know that the two of you came here to the Federal Building this morning?"

"Yes, but that's easily explained," said Palmer. "As a senator, it's nothing unusual for me to come here."

"And the same is true for me," said Canady. "I often

14

have to visit various offices here in connection with my business.''

''All right. I'll come by your place about eight tonight, Mr. Canady.''

Canady stood up. ''We'll be waiting anxiously. And please, Marshal Long, remember . . . discretion.''

There were handshakes all around again, and then Canady and Palmer left the office. When Longarm and Vail heard the outer door close behind them, Vail said, ''Thanks, Custis. I know this is sort of irregular, but . . .''

''But I'm the best man you got,'' Longarm finished with a grin.

Vail flushed. ''Don't let that go to your head. It just so happens all my *real* deputies are out on actual cases right now.''

''Whatever you say, Billy,'' Longarm said, still grinning as he reached for a cheroot.

''One more thing, Custis . . . be careful. I've got sort of a bad feeling about this job.''

Longarm bit down on the cheroot and nodded. ''I know what you mean. Like something about it's not quite right.'' He flicked a lucifer into life with his thumbnail and held the flame to the tip of the cheroot, puffing until it was glowing red. ''But don't you worry. If anybody can find that gal, I'll do it.''

Chapter 3

Henry was the only other person who knew that Canady and Palmer had come to see Vail and Longarm, and Vail swore him to secrecy. Longarm took a closed cab to Canady's mansion that evening, and he kept his snuff-brown Stetson pulled down low over his face as he got out, paid off the driver, and walked through the open gate of the estate.

Canady had bragged on his guards, but Longarm didn't see any of them around tonight. He had only gone a few paces along the gravel drive, however, when a voice sang out from the shadows underneath the trees that dotted the yard.

"Just hold it right there, mister," it said in rough tones that carried the accent of County Cork. "There be three guns pointin' at ye. Who are ye, and what's yer business here?"

"Mr. Canady's expecting me," Longarm said. "My name's Long."

"Aye, that he is. Have ye proof yer who ye say ye are?"

Longarm was carrying his badge and bona fides in their usual leather folder inside his coat, but he hesitated to take them out and display them. He didn't know if the guards were aware that Canady had gone to the Justice Department for help in this matter.

"My word's good," he said bluntly. "Just tell Mr. Canady I'm here."

"We'll do more than that." A bulky figure stepped out of the shadows. The man was tall and wide and wore a derby hat. He gestured with the shotgun he held in blunt-fingered hands and said, "March on up there. We'll let Mr. Canady see ye for his ownself. But I'm warnin' ye . . . try anythin' funny, and I'll use this scattergun to scatter yer innards from here t' Killarney."

Longarm smiled tightly. He had no doubt that this big Irishman meant what he said.

With the guard at his back, Longarm marched on up the drive toward the brightly lit house. It was a massive pile of stone, three stories high, built on a huge lot in the most exclusive neighborhood in Denver. Everybody who lived on this street was either a silver king, a railroad tycoon, a cattle baron, or some other sort of magnate. With the one exception, Longarm reminded himself, of the woman who owned the fanciest, most expensive whorehouse in Denver. She lived in this district too, even though the source of her wealth was down on Colfax Avenue.

As they drew nearer to the house, Longarm glanced back at the man behind him. The guard was only an inch or so shorter than Longarm, and his shoulders were a bit broader. His chest was like a barrel. The growing light revealed a face that had seen more than its share of hard knocks. The features were scarred and lumpy, and the prominent nose had been broken more than once. More like a dozen times, Longarm judged.

The guard had Longarm stand to one side of the front doors while he pulled a bell cord. One of the double doors opened a moment later, and the guard said in his rough voice, "A gent here t' see Mr. Canady. Says he's expected."

A black man with a bald pate and a tonsure of white hair around his ears stepped out of the house. He was wearing a sober black suit and was most likely the butler, Longarm decided. He looked Longarm up and down and then said,

"Indeed. Very well, O'Shaughnessy. You may return to your post now." The butler's accent was British.

"Figgered I'd take him to the boss, I did," the guard said belligerently. "What if he ain't who he says he is? What if he tries t' cause trouble?"

"Then I shall deal with him." The butler's voice was cold and clearly hostile toward O'Shaughnessy.

Longarm was anxious to get inside and get started on the job that had brought him here. It had rankled bad enough just waiting all day to visit Canady's estate. With every minute that passed, the missing Nora could be getting farther away.

"Listen, you two," he said. "Settle your grudge later. I've got important business with Canady, and I intend to see him now." He took a step forward.

Both the guard and the butler shifted slightly, so that they completely blocked the door from Longarm. The friction between them was momentarily forgotten as they closed ranks against the man they regarded as a possible intruder.

"Mr. Long." Canady's voice boomed out in the entrance hall. "I'm glad you're here. Come in, come in."

The butler and the guard moved aside instantly. Longarm stepped between them and into a high-ceilinged foyer. Canady was waiting there. He pumped Longarm's hand and said, "Please, come into my study." He glanced at the butler. "Jennings, bring us some brandy."

"Of course, sir," murmured the butler. He closed the door, and the last glimpse Longarm got of O'Shaughnessy, the big guard was fading back into the shadows.

Nora Canady must have had some sort of secret way out of the estate, to have gotten past a roughneck like that, Longarm thought.

Even with a couple of fancy lamps lit, Canady's study was a dark place. Probably had something to do with those shelves and shelves of heavy, leather-bound books, Longarm decided. He hung his hat on a gold-plated hat tree and sat

18

down in the chair in front of a huge desk while Canady settled down behind it.

"Jonas isn't here this evening," Canady began quietly. "He's left it to me to show you Nora's room. All the reminders of her are rather . . . painful . . . for him."

"I reckon they must be for you too," commented Longarm.

Canady leaned forward and laced his fingers together on the desktop. "Yes, that's certainly true. But Jonas is afraid that some harm has befallen Nora, even though she seems to have left here voluntarily, while I . . . I steadfastly refuse to believe that such a thing is possible. I know that she is all right, and that you will bring her home safely, Marshal Long."

The study door opened behind Longarm as Canady spoke, and the big lawman looked back to see the butler, Jennings, entering the room carrying a silver tray with a decanter and two snifters on it. He set the tray on the desk and began to pour the brandy.

"You can speak freely in front of Jennings, Marshal," Canady went on. "He knows about Nora's disappearance, of course. We couldn't very well keep it from all the servants."

"And I appreciate your trust, Mr. Canady," Jennings said smoothly.

"Hell, yes, I trust you," said Canady. To Longarm, he continued, "Jennings was a freedman working on the railroad with me back in Virginia. We've been together ever since."

"What about O'Shaunnessy?" asked Longarm.

"A gandy dancer while the Union Pacific was being built. I hired him to be in charge of my guards several years ago."

"Does he know about your daughter?"

Canady nodded. "But the other guards don't."

Longarm took the snifter of brandy Jennings handed him. Canady lifted his glass and said, "To the success of your mission."

Longarm nodded and drank. The brandy was like liquid

fire as it slid down his throat and into his belly. He couldn't help but let out a sigh of satisfaction.

"Yes, it is good, isn't it?" Canady's smile was bittersweet. "Money can purchase the finest liquor in the world . . . but sometimes it can't bring back the things that are most precious to us."

Longarm knew the man was talking about his daughter. He took another sip of the brandy, then set the snifter back on the tray. "I need to see Miss Nora's room."

"Of course." Canady set his glass aside and stood up. "I'll take you up myself."

He led the way to a magnificent staircase that curved up from the entrance hall to the second floor. Longarm had been in fancy mansions like this before, but they always made him a little nervous. He couldn't imagine living like this, being surrounded by such luxury day in and day out. He wondered if a fella could even scratch himself in such surroundings without feeling self-conscious about it.

Canady took him along a hallway with a thick rug on the floor and stopped in front of a heavy door. "This is Nora's room," he said as he grasped the knob and turned it. The knob was made out of crystal and gave off a shimmering reflection of the light from the lamps along the hall.

A lamp was lit inside the room too. It sat on a mahogany table next to a big four-poster bed with a silk and lace canopy over it. The rug on the floor in here was even thicker than the one out in the hall. A massive wardrobe sat along one wall, and opposite was a dressing table with a large mirror over it. Another wall was taken up by a spindly-legged divan covered with brocaded upholstery. Two heavy chairs rounded out the furniture. The paper on the walls was decorated with flowery curlicues, and the windows were covered with lace curtains that matched the canopy on the bed. It was undoubtedly a feminine room, yet Longarm thought there was something . . . oppressive . . . about it. The place oozed wealth, but there was still something cold about it. The whole house was that way.

Longarm's eyes were drawn to a painting hung on the wall above the divan. It was a landscape, a golden plain in the foreground, a range of mountains in the background. Longarm recognized the Rockies. He'd seen the view often enough. There was Pikes Peak in the center of the painting, and he figured that the artist must have been down in Colorado Springs when he painted it. Most of Longarm's experience with art consisted of barroom nudes, but something about this picture captured and held his attention.

Canady saw what Longarm was looking at, and said, "Nora's quite talented, I suppose. A shame that nothing will ever come of it."

Longarm looked over at him. "Your daughter painted this?"

"That's right. She's been drawing sketches and painting pictures for as far back as I can remember. Pity that she'll have to give it up when she marries Jonas."

"Give it up?" echoed Longarm. "Why should she do that?"

"Well, painting is hardly a fitting hobby for a senator's wife, is it? Whoever heard of such a thing?"

Longarm shrugged. Just because something was unheard of didn't necessarily mean it was a bad idea. He wasn't going to argue the point with Canady, though. Instead he went over to the wardrobe and paused with his hand on the door, looking back quizzically at Canady.

"Go ahead," Canady said. "I'm sure Nora would be embarrassed to have a strange man pawing through her clothes—but she should have thought of that before she disappeared, shouldn't she?"

"I'll be as careful as I can," Longarm promised.

For the next half hour, he tried to keep that promise as he searched the room for anything that might indicate where Nora Canady had intended to go when she left the mansion. That was assuming, of course, that she'd even had a destination in mind. She might have been in such a hurry to leave that she hadn't cared where she ended up.

21

The time was wasted, however. Longarm didn't find a thing that was suspicious. He looked at Canady, who had watched him in silence, and asked, "Is this the way the room was found?"

"Nothing has been touched," Canady assured him. "At least, there are no signs of . . . of foul play, are there, Marshal?"

"No, there ain't," admitted Longarm. "I'd say you and Senator Palmer are right about Miss Nora leaving on her own, judging from the state of this room leastways. If anybody got in here and grabbed her, there would've been some sign of a struggle."

"So, how will you proceed from here?"

Longarm tried not to sigh. "There are two possibilities, the way I see it. Either your daughter is still here in Denver, or she's not."

Canady nodded and said, "That makes sense."

"If she's here in town somewhere and lying low, she may be harder to find than if she left. I'll have to put the word out and ask a lot of questions—"

"Discreetly, I hope," Canady said, cutting in.

"Discreetly," Longarm agreed with a nod. "I know folks at most of the hotels and boardinghouses in town. I can ask them about Miss Nora without mentioning any names. I'll need to know what she looks like, of course, so I can describe her."

"Of course. I'll give you a complete description, even a photograph. And if she's no longer in Denver?"

"Then she had to leave some way, which means she took a train or a stagecoach or rented a horse or a buggy. Again, that involves pounding a lot of boot leather and asking a heap of questions."

"Well, I'm sure you know what you're doing, Marshal. All I care about are the results." The railroad tycoon's voice cracked a little. "I just want you to find my daughter."

"I'll do my best, Mr. Canady," Longarm assured him. "Now, you said you've got a picture of Miss Nora. . . ."

"Of course. Let's go back downstairs."

Canady led Longarm back to the study, where he took a small, framed photograph from his desk. Longarm had seen the back of it earlier, but Canady hadn't turned it around so that Longarm could see the subject of the picture. Now Canady handed it to him, and Longarm took it and studied it.

The sepia-toned photograph was of a young woman in a high-necked dress, looking solemn as folks usually did when they had their pictures made. Her hair was thick and piled into an elaborate arrangement of curls on her well-shaped head. Her mouth was a trifle too big for her to be considered classically beautiful, but something about her—those large, dark, luminous eyes maybe—hit Longarm like a punch in the belly. Nora Canady was the most flat-out attractive female he had seen in quite a spell.

Longarm swallowed and asked, "How old is your daughter?"

"She just turned twenty," answered Canady.

"Mighty pretty."

"She means the world to me, Marshal."

Longarm had already promised Canady he would do his best. He didn't feel like repeating the pledge. Instead he hefted the photograph and said, "I'll take good care of this and won't show it to nobody unless I just have to. I know you want to keep this quiet."

"Thank you, Marshal. I appreciate your understanding, and I know Jonas does too." Canady must have sensed that the meeting was over, because he began showing Longarm out of the study. "When will you begin your investigation?" he asked as they walked through the big entrance hall.

"Right away," said Longarm. "It's early yet. I'll do a little work tonight."

"I couldn't ask for a better effort than that." Canady shook hands with Longarm again at the front door. "Good night, Marshal."

Longarm bid the railroad tycoon good night and started walking down the long drive toward the street. He might be

23

able to catch a cab, he thought, but if he didn't, he could hoof it back downtown. He'd done enough cowboying in his younger years, after his service in the Late Unpleasantness, so that he didn't care much for walking, but the night air was pleasant and he didn't mind the prospect of a stroll that awful much.

O'Shaughnessy was waiting at the front gate, which had been closed since Longarm's arrival. The guard swung the wrought-iron gate open and said, "Good night to ye, Mr. Long."

"Good night, Mr. O'Shaughnessy," Longarm replied.

The gate closed behind him with a loud clang.

Longarm looked one way, then the other, along the deserted street. There were no hansom cabs in sight, no buggies, no riders, no pedestrians other than him. That struck him as a little odd, but he didn't give it much thought as he started walking east toward Denver's downtown district.

He had gone about a hundred yards when the rumble of wheels on paving stones made him glance over his shoulder. A large wagon had entered the street from somewhere. He saw it clearly as it passed beneath one of the gas streetlights. The wagon was loaded with barrels and drawn by a fine team of matched black horses, six of them in all.

Six black horses, thought Longarm wryly. That was the number and color of the team that traditionally pulled hearses. This was no undertaker's wagon coming toward him, however. It was just a tradesman's vehicle of some sort.

That thought was going through Longarm's head when the driver suddenly slapped his reins down on the backs of his team and called out to them. The black horses surged forward against their harness, breaking into a gallop and pulling the wagon along behind them at breakneck speed.

It took Longarm a second to realize that the horses were coming straight at him.

Chapter 4

Longarm hadn't survived so long by being slow when it counted. His instincts took over and flung him to one side as the horses and wagon thundered down on him.

He landed hard on the paving stones, bruising his right shoulder. His momentum carried him on over in a roll that brought him up on his knees. In the glow from a streetlight, he caught a glimpse of the teamster's face as the wagon raced past him. The man was bearded, but that was all Longarm could tell about him. He had a floppy-brimmed hat pulled down tight on his head, shielding the rest of his features.

"Hey!" Longarm shouted. The wagon never slowed down. Longarm felt like drawing his gun and sending a couple of slugs after the son of a bitch, but he stopped with his fingers just touching the polished walnut grips of the Colt. Being careless wasn't really a crime, and Billy Vail didn't much like it when his deputies went around town discharging their weapons at the citizens of Denver.

Longarm stood up, started to brush himself off, then grimaced as a pungent odor struck his nose. He lifted his left arm, sniffed at the sleeve of his coat, and made an even worse face. He had rolled right through a pile of horse apples.

"Shit!" he said, both appropriately and emphatically.

Well, at least it was a warm night, he told himself, trying

25

to take a philosophical bent as he stripped off the coat and rolled it into a ball after taking the small, framed photograph of Nora Canady from the breast pocket.

In shirtsleeves, vest, and string tie, he strode on down the street. He would stop at the Chinese laundry he normally used—old Chow would still be there, despite the lateness of the hour—and drop off the coat to be cleaned. Then he could proceed on his mission.

It would be nice, thought Longarm, to run into that wagon driver again and teach him a little lesson. But the likelihood of that was mighty slim, especially considering the fact that Longarm hadn't gotten a good enough look at him to recognize him again. What had happened tonight was going to be one of those little injustices of life that never got avenged, Longarm told himself.

Half an hour later, after leaving the soiled coat with the Chinese laundryman, Longarm strolled into one of Denver's nicer hotels. The desk clerk knew him and gave him a pleasant nod of greeting. The lobby was almost empty. A couple of men sat in armchairs on the other side of the room, reading newspapers. Other than the clerk, they were the only people in sight.

Longarm crossed the lobby to the desk and said, "Evenin', Carl. Quiet night?"

"It's always quiet here, Marshal. Our guests insist upon it. What can I do for you?"

"I'm looking for a lady."

The clerk nodded knowingly. "Yes, I'd heard about your, ah, romantic troubles, Marshal. You have my deepest sympathy and my hopes that the situation soon resolves itself."

"Dad blast it!" snapped Longarm. "Word gets around this town too fast. Don't you boys have anything better to do than gossip?"

"I meant no offense, Marshal," the clerk said hastily. "I'm sure one of the bellboys can find a lady who would be glad to keep you company this evening."

Wearily, Longarm rubbed a hand over his face, then put his palms on the desk and leaned forward. "That ain't what I'm looking for," he said between gritted teeth. "I'm looking for one certain lady, and it's business I want with her, not pleasure."

"Oh. I'm sorry for the misunderstanding."

Longarm waved off the apology. "This woman I'm after would have arrived last Saturday night maybe. No earlier than that, but it could have been sometime since then. She's about twenty years old, dresses well, and is mighty pretty."

"Do you know her name?" asked the clerk.

"I don't know what name she might've been using," Longarm answered, which was true as far as it went.

"Well, it doesn't really matter, since I'm afraid I can't help you, Marshal. We have no single female guests at the moment, and there haven't been any since well before this past Saturday."

Longarm had been afraid of that. But this was only the first step on what might turn out to be a long trail. He nodded and said, "Much obliged anyway."

"Do you want me to keep an eye out for this woman, Marshal?"

"I'd appreciate it. And if you could sort of pass the word along to the fellas who work the other shifts . . ."

"Of course."

"But other than that, keep it under your hat. Make sure the other clerks know that too."

"Absolutely," the clerk assured Longarm. "You can count on us for discretion, Marshal." He gave a smile that was half-smirk. "After all, our profession demands it."

Longarm thanked the man again and moved on. There were several more hotels in downtown Denver that he intended to visit tonight. The boardinghouses would have to wait until the next day.

For the next hour, Longarm walked from hotel to hotel, asking the same questions. In each case, he failed to get the results he wanted. Either there were no single females staying at the places, or they were too old to be the one he was looking for. By the time he gave up for the night and headed back to his own rented room, he was frustrated and ready to start wondering if maybe he was on the wrong track.

Nothing said that Nora Canady had to have gone to a hotel alone, he told himself. Maybe she had a lover. Maybe that was why she had run off instead of marrying Jonas Palmer. She could be in a hotel room right now with some lucky fella, romping to beat the band.

Or she could have disguised herself to look older, Longarm speculated. That was more far-fetched, but not beyond the realm of possibility. He had been asking about a twenty-year-old woman, when all along Nora might have made herself look twice that old. But why would she have done such a thing?

That was the question that all the other questions came back to, he realized. Nora must have had a damned good reason to disappear. If Longarm could figure out what that reason was, he might be a lot closer to discovering where she was now.

But he'd have to ponder on that tomorrow, he decided as he chewed on an unlit cheroot and crossed the wooden bridge that spanned Cherry Creek. His rooming house was close by. In the quiet night, his boot heels rang loudly on the planks of the bridge.

A shape moved out of the shadows at the far end of the bridge.

"Hold it right there, mister."

Longarm stopped in his tracks as the voice barked the order at him. He didn't stop because he was frightened, since he wasn't. He came to a halt because he wanted to find out what this shadowy hombre was up to. He supposed he was just naturally curious.

The familiar ratcheting of a gun being cocked came to his ears. Then the voice said, "Keep your hands where I can see 'em."

Longarm raised his arms and held his hands out to the

sides. "This a holdup, fella?" he asked. "If it is, you've picked the wrong time of the month. Payday ain't for a couple of weeks yet, and I'm already down to the bottom of the barrel."

That was true enough. He had been thinking of paying a visit to the Denver Public Library, not only because of the friendly gal who worked there, but also because sitting around and reading was a cheap way to pass the time.

The shadowy figure came closer, stepping out onto the bridge itself. "Don't give me that," the man snarled. He poked something toward Longarm. "Hand over the loot, or I'll blow a hole clean through you, mister."

Longarm sighed. The would-be robber was about ten feet from him, which was close enough for what Longarm had in mind. "Look, I'll give you my watch, all right?"

"Just make it fast!"

Longarm reached for the chain that looped across his midsection from one vest pocket to the other. At one end of the chain was a heavy gold pocket watch shaped like a turnip. But at the other end, its weight counterbalancing that of the watch and acting as a fob, was a two-shot .44 derringer that had saved Longarm's life on numerous occasions. He wasn't sure how much danger his life was actually in at the moment, but the holdup artist did have a gun. Longarm wasn't of a mind to take too many chances under those circumstances.

But he wasn't going to just gun the man down without warning either. He pulled on the watch chain with his left hand, and as the derringer came out of his vest pocket it slipped nice and natural into his right. He thrust it out, his thumb looping over the hammer and earing it back as he did so. The robber jumped a little and exclaimed, "What the hell!"

"It's called a .44-caliber over-and-under two-shot, old son," drawled Longarm. "And it'll blow a hole clean through *you* if you don't put up that hogleg and skedaddle out of here."

"What . . . but . . . but I've got five bullets in this gun!"

"I don't need but one," said Longarm.

He was prepared to stand there for however long it took for the standoff to be resolved. The robber had to realize that his intended victim had teeth after all and didn't intend to be held up. The simplest thing would be to fade back into the darkness and be grateful he was still alive.

The gun being held by the shadowy figure began to droop toward the bridge. "All right, all right," he muttered. "Hell, a man can't even make a dishonest living in this town anymore."

"Now you're being smart," Longarm told him.

The robber stuck his gun back in his coat, turned, and trudged away. Longarm watched him go, and kept the derringer trained on him until the shadows reclaimed him.

Longarm put away the derringer, but immediately palmed out his Colt and held it alongside his leg as he started off the bridge. There was a chance the holdup man had really taken his advice and gone home, wherever that was, but it was just as likely that the fella was still lying in wait for him. And there wouldn't be any warning this time, just a shot from ambush.

Well, there was a little bit of warning, Longarm reflected as he reached the end of the bridge. He heard the soft scrape of a footstep nearby.

He threw himself to the left as a gun roared. His left hand grabbed the railing of the bridge and he swung himself around it onto the embankment leading down to the creek. The corner of the bridge wasn't much cover, but it was the best available at the moment. Another shot banged, and this time Longarm got a good look at the muzzle flash as the slug chewed a splinter from the bridge railing a foot from his head. He fired at the flash, responding so quickly that the two shots sounded almost like one.

Something hit the ground over there, catty-cornered across the road. Longarm crouched by the end of the bridge and waited to see if there were going to be any more shots. In the distance, a dog started barking, and that set off a dozen more mutts. But those were the only sounds Longarm heard.

Until a moment later when a soft, rasping noise reached his ears. Somebody was struggling to breathe. A few more seconds passed, and the breathing turned into a groan of pain.

That could have been faked to try to draw him out, but when the breathing resumed, it had a bubbling quality to it. After a moment, Longarm heard a ghastly rattle. He had heard similar sounds many times in the past, and nobody had ever been able to fake one of those.

He straightened and stepped up off the embankment, holding his Colt ready just in case as he started across the road. When he reached the far side, near where the shots had come from, he dug out a lucifer and held it out at arm's length in his left hand before snapping his iron-hard thumbnail against the head. The match flared into life. Longarm squinted from the glare as he looked down at the body sprawled at his feet.

The man was lying face-down in a spreading pool of blood. His gun lay a few feet away, near an outstretched hand. Also lying on the street was a broad-brimmed hat. Longarm pointed the Colt down at the fallen figure as he worked the toe of his boot under the man's arm. He rolled the corpse over and stepped back quickly.

The man was dead, all right. Longarm lit another match and saw that his bullet had gone through the right side of the man's chest, undoubtedly puncturing a lung so that he had drowned on his own blood. Plenty of the crimson stuff had leaked out of him, that was for sure. Longarm saw something else that made him frown.

The fella had a beard—a bushy, black beard just like the driver of the wagon that had nearly run over him earlier tonight.

And that hat lying near the corpse . . . it was the same sort of hat that teamster had worn, Longarm recalled.

Of course, there were probably hundreds of hats just like that in Denver, just as there were thousands of men in town who wore beards. Just because this fella had such a hat, and such a beard, didn't necessarily mean that he was the same man who had tried to crush Longarm beneath the wheels of a heavily loaded wagon.

Didn't mean he *wasn't* either.

Longarm knelt beside the corpse and quickly searched the man's pockets. He drew a roll of blood-soaked bills from inside the coat. Without counting them, he could tell from the thickness of the roll that the man hadn't been poor. That sort of blew holes in the robbery theory. This gent had pretended to be a holdup man, but his real goal had been something else entirely.

He had been out to kill Longarm, plain and simple.

Then why go to the trouble of making it look and sound like a robbery? Longarm asked himself as he stood up. Why not just a shot out of the dark? Then he answered his own questions by realizing that the would-be killer must have been following orders in that respect as well. Someone had told the man to get rid of Longarm, but to make it appear to be a botched holdup, just in case there were any witnesses. Just as the earlier attempt on his life with the wagon would have looked like an accident if anyone had investigated it.

Interesting. Mighty interesting. So interesting that Longarm thought about it for a long time after leaving the body where it was and returning to his room to try to get some sleep that wouldn't come.

Chapter 5

"The Denver police found a body down by the Cherry Creek bridge last night," Billy Vail said as he looked across his desk at Longarm the next morning.

Longarm didn't look up at his boss until after he finished lighting his first cheroot of the day. Then he said casually, "Is that so?"

"Yes, it is. You wouldn't know anything about that, would you, Custis?"

He should have waited with the body for a policeman to show up, thought Longarm. But he hadn't been in any mood for a bunch of questions and paperwork. The bearded man was just as dead either way.

"Why would I know anything about a corpse, Billy?" he asked blandly.

"Because this fella was a friend of an old friend of yours. A former cell mate, in fact. You remember Bob McGurk?"

Longarm's eyebrows arched in surprise. "Badger Bob?"

"One and the same," said Vail. "The dead man's name was Ross. He spent three years in Leavenworth with McGurk. Ross was in for mail robbery. Got out about six months ago."

"Badger Bob's still in there, ain't he?"

"He's supposed to be." Vail looked intently at Longarm.

"He escaped two weeks ago when he was out on a work detail. Killed two guards doing it."

"Damn it!" Longarm leaned forward. "Didn't those folks at Leavenworth have sense enough to know not to ever let Bob out of his hole?"

"Evidently not."

Longarm sat back in his chair and took a deep draw on the cheroot as he remembered his first run-in with Badger Bob McGurk. It had happened not long after he'd gone to work for the Justice Department. McGurk had held up an army payroll wagon all by his lonesome, had killed four soldiers and wounded four more in the process. Then, while Longarm was trying to track him down, he had gone on a killing spree, murdering six more people before Longarm caught up with him in an isolated Idaho canyon. The two dead guards at Leavenworth brought his total number of victims to an even dozen, assuming that Badger Bob hadn't killed any other prisoners while he was there. Given the man's record, it was a wonder he hadn't been hanged, but he'd been lucky and drawn a judge who decided to sentence him to life in prison instead. Longarm had a feeling that was because the army payroll Bob had stolen had never been found, and the government probably still held out faint hopes of getting him to talk someday so that they could recover the money.

Longarm could have told them that wasn't going to happen. Badger Bob was one of the craziest bastards Longarm had ever run across. He would have gnawed off his own arms before he'd cooperate with the law about anything.

"I didn't know McGurk was on the loose," Longarm said slowly.

Vail nodded. "And you're one of the men he swore he'd get even with, Custis."

"You say this fella Ross used to be his cell mate?"

"That's right. Ross—the man who was killed last night down by Cherry Creek."

Longarm chewed on his cheroot, shifting it from one side

of his mouth to the other. This bit of information might put things in a whole new light. He had formed a hazy theory as to why the bearded man might have wanted to kill him, but knowing that the fella was connected to Badger Bob McGurk provided Longarm with a much simpler explanation for the attempt on his life. And the simplest explanation, he had learned over the years, was usually the best.

"This gent Ross . . . had he been on the straight and narrow since getting out of prison?"

"Not hardly," said Vail. "He'd been picked up several times by the Denver police for getting drunk and starting fights, and he was a suspect in a handful of robberies and assaults. They even thought he might have killed a couple of folks, but nobody had any proof."

"Well, it sounds like whoever ventilated the bastard did the world a favor. No need for him to be wasting perfectly good air by breathing it."

Vail inclined his head. "You could look at it that way."

"Then why don't we?" suggested Longarm.

Vail sighed in defeat. "All right, if that's the way you want it. Anyway, the real problem is McGurk. He's liable to be after you, Custis."

Longarm shook his head and said, "I'm not afraid of ol' Badger Bob."

"Well, you should be," snapped Vail. "You ought to be worried a little anyway. The man's murdered at least a dozen people, and he's about as vicious a killer as I've ever seen."

"He is all of that," agreed Longarm.

"I've put the word out to all of our men to keep an eye open for McGurk, and I've warned the Denver police too." The chief marshal shrugged. "I don't know what else I can do."

"There isn't anything else." Longarm stood up, stretching his rangy frame. "If McGurk comes after me, I'll deal with him then."

"Just be careful." Longarm started to turn away, and Vail added hurriedly, "Hey, what about that Canady girl? I figured that was why you came in this morning, to report on that investigation.''

Longarm nodded. ''I went to Canady's house last night, had a look around the place. It doesn't seem likely to me that somebody could have gotten in there and snatched the gal, Billy. I have to agree with Canady and Senator Palmer that she probably left on her own. Seems to me that even that would have been hard, though, with the guards Canady has around the place.''

''Then you haven't located any sign of her?''

''Nary a one. I checked some of the hotels last night, figured I'd hit the rest of them and the boardinghouses this morning. If that doesn't turn up anything, I'll start looking into the possibility that she left Denver altogether.''

''Hell, if she did, she could have gone anywhere,'' Vail grumbled.

Longarm nodded. ''I'm afraid you're right, Billy. That's what makes this one bitch of a job.''

And now he had to worry about a lunatic like Badger Bob McGurk on top of it.

The morning was as unproductive as the night before had been. He checked the rest of the hotels, including some dives that Nora Canady likely wouldn't have been caught dead in, and moved on to the boardinghouses. No one had seen a young woman matching Nora's description.

But at least nobody tried to kill him, and Longarm was thankful for that.

After eating lunch in a hash house, Longarm headed for the railroad depot. He was friends with several of the ticket agents, and by talking with them, he discovered that, again, no one answering Nora Canady's description had purchased a ticket during the past few days. ''But that doesn't mean she couldn't have boarded a train and bought a ticket from the conductor after it pulled out,'' one of the agents advised Longarm, which nearly brought a groan of despair from the big lawman. Without a good starting place, Denver—and the whole sweep of the frontier beyond it—made for a mighty big area in which to be searching for one young woman. Longarm had heard the old saying about the needle and the haystack, and he was starting to understand just what it meant.

Faced with a dwindling supply of options, Longarm began making the rounds of the stagecoach companies. Several of them maintained offices in Denver, and he checked with each in turn. With so many railroads criss-crossing the country these days, the stage lines didn't do as much business as they once had, but they still carried quite a few passengers to the places the railroads didn't reach.

It was late afternoon before Longarm got the first lucky break that had come along in this case.

He was in the office of the Richter, Gramlich & Burke Stagecoach Company, one of the smaller outfits, talking to a ticket agent named Waterman. Longarm described Nora Canady, and before he was even finished, the young man was nodding.

"Yes, sir," said Waterman, "that sounds like a lady who came in here early Sunday morning and bought a ticket for Raton."

"How early?"

"It was right after we opened up, if I recall correctly. About eight o'clock."

Just on general principles, Longarm tried not to let the agent see this news affected him. "When did the stage for Raton leave?"

"Nine o'clock, on the dot. We may be one of the smaller operations, but we stick to our schedule," Waterman added proudly.

Longarm reached into his coat—not the one he'd gotten dirty rolling in the street the night before—and slid the framed photograph of Nora Canady from the inside pocket where he had been carrying it all day. He'd planned to be careful about showing it around, holding it in reserve until he got a strong nibble such as the one he had now. He turned

37

it so that Waterman could see the picture and asked, "Is this the lady?"

An admiring grin split the young man's face. "It sure is. I wouldn't forget somebody that pretty."

Longarm put the photograph away, causing Waterman to look slightly disappointed. "How long does it take that stage to get to Raton?" Longarm asked.

"It's a three-day run."

That would have put Nora into Raton late in the day on Tuesday. This was Thursday. She had a good lead on him, but if she was still in Raton, he could catch up to her without too much trouble. Assuming she had even taken the stage and not just bought a ticket to throw any pursuers off the trail.

"You saw her get on the stage yourself?"

"Yes, sir. I put her bag in the boot for her."

"Where does that stage go from Raton?"

"On down to Tucumcari and then into Texas to Fort Stockton."

"Rugged country down that way," said Longarm.

"Yes, sir. But I hear that the Texas & Pacific is building in that direction, and once the railroad goes through, all that part of Texas will get civilized in a hurry."

Longarm grinned. "Civilization never gets in a hurry in Texas, old son," he said.

He hoped Nora was still in Raton. The town was just over the border from Colorado in New Mexico Territory, in the Sangre de Cristo Mountains. Longarm knew it well, knew that if Nora was still there, he would probably be able to find her fairly easily. The problem was that from Raton, she would have been able to head southeast into Texas or southwest toward Santa Fe and Albuquerque.

The haystack had gotten smaller, but Nora Canady was still a needle.

Longarm thanked the young ticket agent and headed back to the railroad station. The Atchison, Topeka & Santa Fe could get him to Raton considerably quicker than the Richter,

Gramlich & Burke stage line. He was grateful to Waterman for the help, but gratitude only went so far. Right now, speed was more important.

He went ahead and purchased his ticket, knowing that Billy Vail would reimburse him later. Vail got his dander up about some of the expense vouchers Longarm turned in, but he wasn't likely to complain about this one.

The southbound train wasn't due to arrive for another hour, which gave Longarm plenty of time to stop by the Federal Building. Henry ushered him into the chief marshal's office right away.

Vail looked up eagerly. "Find anything, Custis?"

"Maybe," said Longarm. "I talked to a fella who works for one of the stage lines. He says Nora Canady bought a ticket to Raton early Sunday morning. He put her on the coach himself."

Vail slapped a palm down on the scarred wooden top of the desk. "Good! I reckon you're on your way down there now?"

"Train leaves in less than an hour," Longarm confirmed. "All I've got to do first is stop by my place and pick up a few possibles."

"You've got your ticket already?"

Longarm nodded.

"Good," Vail said again. "Talk to Henry on your way out. He'll pay you back for the ticket and give you some more expense money. Whatever you need on this one, Custis, no questions asked."

Longarm frowned as he eased a cheroot from his vest pocket. "Why're you going all out like this, Billy?" he asked. "It ain't like you to get your fur in an uproar over what some politician wants."

Vail didn't look offended at the blunt question. He and Longarm had known each other for too many years, ridden too many of the same trails, for him to object. His reply was equally blunt.

"Senator Palmer's an important man in Washington,"

Vail said. "Word is, he's in line for a committee chairmanship that'll put him in a position to send more funding our way."

"Money?" said Longarm with a snort. "This is about money?"

As soon as he spoke, he knew he had been too hasty. Billy Vail wasn't the hardcase he had once been, true enough. His hair was thinning and his belly had grown some since he'd taken to riding a desk instead of a horse. But as he looked up at Longarm and scowled, his eyes flashed with the same fire that had scared the piss out of scores of lawbreakers in years past.

"Damn it, Custis," he said in a low, dangerous voice, "you think I *like* having to bitch about expenses and watch every penny my men spend? The more funding this office gets, the better prepared all of you deputies are when I send you to risk your lives. I want all you boys to have the best horses, the finest guns, and all the ammunition you could ever need." He shoved some papers aside brusquely. "Besides, I saw the look in Bryce Canady's eyes when he told us about his daughter being gone. It didn't matter then who he is or how much money and power he has. He was just a daddy who was hurting because he didn't know what had happened to his little girl. That's the sort of man I want to help."

Longarm was a little embarrassed by what he had said earlier. He covered it by saying, "Well, hell, Billy, you didn't have to go to speechifying. I knew better."

"Good." Vail waved a hand. "Now get out of here, and go find that young woman before something bad happens to her."

Longarm nodded. "That's just what I plan to do."

But as he turned away, he thought of all the dangers in the world and hoped that he wasn't already too late.

Chapter 6

On his way back to the depot, Longarm stopped by his rented room and picked up his Winchester, his carpetbag with a couple of changes of clothes and a box of .44 cartridges in it, and his McClellan saddle. While he hoped that Nora Canady was still in Raton, it was always possible he would have to do some horsebacking before this job was over.

The southbound was on time. It was early evening when the locomotive eased out of the depot and began building up speed. By the next morning it would be in Raton. Longarm was sitting up in one of the coaches, which was where he would be spending the night. All the other accommodations had already been booked.

That was all right, he told himself as he sat and smoked and watched the twilight gathering over the plains outside the window of the coach. He had slept sitting up plenty of times before. In fact, he was just about to doze off when he felt someone sit down on the bench beside him.

He looked around, tensing slightly because he hadn't forgotten about the threat to his life represented by Badger Bob McGurk. The person sitting beside him was no crazy, murderous outlaw, however. Instead, she was a sweet-looking young woman with brunette curls peeking out from beneath her bonnet.

Longarm reached up and tugged on the brim of his Stetson. "Ma'am," he said politely.

"Good evening to you, sir," she replied. "I do so hope you are a gentleman."

Longarm couldn't help but chuckle. "I try to be," he said dryly.

"Excellent. A young lady traveling alone can't be too careful, you know."

"So I've heard. My name's Custis Long." Then, to ease her mind a little, he added, "I'm a U.S. deputy marshal."

"A marshal!" the woman exclaimed. "Then I really *am* safe in my choice of traveling companions, aren't I?"

Some would have disagreed with that, thought Longarm. In fact, under the circumstances, being around him might not be that safe at all. Someone had tried to kill him a couple of times the night before, after all.

But he didn't say that to this young woman, just reminded her, "You haven't told me your name."

"Oh, of course. I apologize for my rudeness. I'm Miss Toplin, Emily Toplin."

Longarm touched the brim of his hat again. "Pleased to meet you, Miss Toplin."

"Where are you bound, Marshal, if you don't mind my asking?"

Even in the shadows of the coach, which was lit only by a couple of lamps, Longarm could tell that her eyes were a luminous blue. "Don't mind at all, ma'am," he said. "I'm going down to Raton. What about you?"

"I'm going to Santa Fe." She paused, then added, "To join my fiancé."

"Oh," said Longarm.

Well, he hadn't really figured on making any advances to her anyway, he told himself. She was about as wholesome as a week-old pup, and while he knew from experience that such innocent exteriors sometimes hid downright lustful interiors, he figured that wasn't the case here. Besides, he was only going to be on the train for about twelve hours.

"Is your trip to Raton for business or pleasure, Marshal?" she asked. "Are you going down there to arrest some desperado?"

"Nope," Longarm replied with a grin. "I don't plan on arresting nobody."

"Then you're traveling for pleasure."

"I hope so," he said. It would be a pleasure to locate Nora Canady and find out what this whole affair was all about, he thought.

Miss Emily Toplin was the talkative sort, Longarm discovered. She chattered on as the train rolled southward, requiring little from him other than an occasional muttered comment to show that he was still listening. After a while, though, she wound down and started yawning.

"I wish I could have gotten a sleeping berth," she said. "I'm not sure I can sleep sitting up like this."

"It's an acquired skill," Longarm told her as he leaned back and tipped his hat down over his eyes. "Luckily, I've had a lot of practice at it."

He had hoped his gesture would quiet her down, and sure enough, it did. In fact, she dozed off before he did, and as the train swung around a bend, she slid toward him, her head coming to rest against his shoulder as she snuggled next to him.

Longarm sighed. Looked like he was going to sleep with this gal after all . . . just not quite the way he had first thought.

While he waited to fall asleep, he mulled over the case that had brought him here. He had realized that in concentrating on how Nora Canady could have disappeared and where she might have gone, he had neglected to think much about what he would do once he found her. Her father and Senator Palmer would be expecting him to bring her back to Denver. Billy Vail seemed to have taken that for granted too.

But ducking out just before a wedding was no crime, and neither was running away from home. What he had told Emily Toplin was the truth: He didn't expect to arrest anybody in Raton, even if he found Nora there.

Maybe she'd had a good reason for leaving Denver. Bryce Canady hadn't struck Longarm as a brutal man, but who knows what went on behind closed doors? The same was true of Jonas Palmer. Just because he was a senator with a good reputation didn't mean he wasn't a gold-plated son of a bitch in private. If any of that speculation turned out to be true, how could Longarm, in all good conscience, force Nora to go back to Denver?

The answer was simple. He couldn't.

He sighed. Further along he'd know more about it, as the old hymn went. Until then, he would just do the job he had been given, which was to find Nora Canady.

Emily Toplin shifted slightly, and so did Longarm, thinking that the young woman was uncomfortable. Something tugged at his coat. He heard a soft noise.

He looked down and saw the small, sharp knife blade that had cut right through his coat and pinned the material to the wooden seat back.

A yell of surprise was jolted out of him by the realization that Emily had just tried to kill him. She exploded into motion, demonstrating clearly that she hadn't been asleep at all, only shamming. The heel of her left hand cracked against Longarm's jaw, jerking his head back. Emily's other hand dove into her reticule and came out with a little pistol.

Longarm lunged, trying to grab her wrist before she could fire, but the way his coat was stuck to the seat by the knife hampered his movements. He managed to bat the gun to the side as she pulled the trigger. The pistol gave a wicked little crack, and the bullet whipped past Longarm's head and smacked through the window beside him.

By now the struggle and the gunshot had attracted a lot of attention from the other occupants of the crowded coach. Emily screamed, "Help me! Someone help me!" as she tried to bring the gun to bear on Longarm again.

He ripped his coat loose and grabbed her wrist, forcing

44

the gun toward the floor. Emily screeched like he was killing her. "He's a monster!" she howled. "He tried to molest me!"

A man who had been sitting behind them leaned over the seat and grabbed Longarm's shoulder. "Hold on there, fella!" he said. "What the hell do you think you're doing to that young lady?"

Trying to keep her from killing me, thought Longarm, but he didn't waste any breath putting it into words. He saw the look in Emily's eyes as she panted and struggled with him. She wanted to see him dead. He shook off the grip of the man behind him and gave Emily a hard shove, sending her sliding off the bench seat. She sat down hard in the aisle. Longarm loomed over her as he wrested the pistol from her fingers.

"Look out!" somebody yelled. "He's got a gun!"

Damn it, now one of these pilgrims was liable to panic and start shooting at him. He straightened, holding his hands up in plain sight, and bellowed, "Everybody shut up! I'm a U.S. marshal!"

Emily, who was lying in the aisle at his feet, kicked him in the groin as hard as she could.

It felt like a cannon going off between Longarm's legs. He bit back a curse and bent almost double, curling around the pain that suddenly filled him. His right hand caught hold of a seat back, and that was all that held him up. He was vaguely aware of hands clutching at him, probably belonging to the passengers who thought he was somehow to blame for all this. He wanted to shake them off, but at the moment, he just didn't have the strength.

Emily rolled over onto her hands and knees, then came up on her feet. She was facing away from him, and she broke into a run, pushing through the crowd that had gathered around them. People got out of her way, most likely because they thought she was running away from the man who had threatened her. Longarm lifted his head and stared blearily after her, seeing her disappear through the door at the rear of the coach.

The agony in his crotch was subsiding a little now, and he was able to straighten up and reach inside his coat for the leather folder that contained his badge and bona fides. He opened it and held it up so that the angry passengers could see the lamplight reflect off the badge. "I'm a lawman, damn it!" he grated as he started trying to shove his way through the press of people. "Let me by!"

The crowd finally began to part again, and he stumbled through the path that created toward the back of the coach. He became aware that the train was slowing down. Had they reached a scheduled stop already?

The door through which Emily had vanished opened again just before Longarm could reach it. The blue-suited conductor stepped through, calling, "Castle Rock! Castle Rock!" He was obviously unaware of the disturbance that had taken place in this car, but he stopped short, a look of surprise on his pudgy face, when he saw the passengers standing in the aisle and the big, grim-faced lawman coming toward him.

"Did you see her?" snapped Longarm.

"See who?" the conductor asked, wide-eyed.

"A young woman. She just ran out of here."

"Sorry, mister. I didn't see anybody like that."

With a jolt and a hiss of brakes, the train came to a halt. Longarm looked out at a long station platform beside the tracks. The train had been going slowly enough as it eased into the station that Emily could have jumped off without risking an injury. Longarm stepped out onto the small platform at the rear of the coach and gripped the railing that ran around it. The hour was late, and the town of Castle Rock was dark for the most part. Emily could have been anywhere. He would be wasting his time trying to find her.

"Say, I know you," the conductor said. "You're the one they call Longarm."

"Yeah," admitted Longarm.

Some of the passengers had come to the door of the coach.

46

One of them pointed a finger at Longarm and said to the conductor, "That man tried to molest a young woman!"

"That's a damned lie," Longarm said. "She was trying to kill me."

"After you took liberties with her." The passenger, who wore the tweed suit and bowler hat of a drummer of some kind, sneered at Longarm. "We all saw it."

Longarm swung sharply toward the man, trying not to wince as the movement made fresh pain cascade through his groin. "You didn't see anything of the sort, mister. Come on."

He shouldered past the passengers and stalked down the aisle toward the bench where he and Emily had been sitting. The knife was still there, its point buried in the wood of the seat back.

Longarm pointed at the weapon and said, "That gal was pretending to be asleep; then she tried to put that pigsticker between my ribs."

The knife still had a small, torn piece of fabric from Longarm's coat pinned to the wood. The conductor bent over, studied it, then straightened and nodded to Longarm. "Looks like she tried to stick you, all right. But what were you doin' to her at the time?"

"Nothing!" Longarm ground his teeth in exasperation. "I thought she was asleep. I damned near was too. It was just luck that made me shift a mite, so that she missed with the knife."

The conductor rubbed his jaw. "Hard to believe a young woman would try to kill a man for no reason."

"Maybe . . ." Longarm's brain worked furiously. "Maybe she was dreaming, having a nightmare. She thought somebody was trying to hurt her, so she lashed out at the fella who happened to be closest to her at the time—me."

It was a plausible explanation, Longarm supposed, but he didn't really believe it. He had seen the look in Emily's eyes. There was something more to this attempt on his life. Longarm was sure of it.

The conductor seemed to have bought the line of bull Longarm had handed him, however. "In that case, I reckon you're lucky you weren't hurt, Marshal. But why did the young lady run off, and where did she go?"

Longarm could only shake his head. "I don't know."

"Well, I'll have a word with the town marshal while we're stopped here and tell him to be watching for her. We can't wait until she comes to her senses. That would throw us off schedule."

"Wouldn't want that," Longarm said sincerely.

And thank goodness for the almighty schedule of the Atchison, Topeka & Santa Fe, he added to himself. When the train pulled out again in a few minutes, the mysterious and murderous Emily Toplin wouldn't be on it, so that would be one less threat Longarm would have to worry about tonight.

He pulled the knife out of the seat back and gave it to the conductor, then sat down and pulled his coat around so that he could look at the hole torn in it. He sighed. The past couple of days had been hard on his coats, that was for damned sure. He didn't have an extra one with him, so he'd just have to wear this one with a rip in it.

Longarm took out a cheroot, lit it, sat back, and frowned. The other passengers had all returned to their seats, but some of them were still casting hostile, suspicious glances in his direction. The pain in his balls had faded to a dull ache, but he figured it would be with him for a few days. He sure as hell wouldn't be up to any tomcatting around . . . not that he'd have time for such activities anyway.

Three attempts on his life in twenty-four hours. That was a lot, even for him. The two by the bearded man called Ross could be explained away by Ross's connection with Badger Bob McGurk. But what was he to make of Emily Toplin? Longarm didn't believe she had roused from the depths of a nightmare and, thinking it was real, struck out at the handiest target. No, she had known exactly what she was doing, he decided. She had wanted him dead, no two ways about it.

But why?

He sighed and chewed on the cheroot, knowing that he was facing another night of unanswered questions and long-delayed slumber.

Chapter 7

The sun had been up for about an hour when the train came through the pass in the mountains that marked the border between Colorado and New Mexico Territory and slid down the long grade into the town of Raton. The settlement was, by and large, a cattle town, serving the vast ranches here in the northeast corner of the territory. Longarm had visited Raton many times before, and when he swung down from the train car, his long-legged strides carried him through the depot and down the street toward the local office of the Richter, Gramlich & Burke Stagecoach Company.

He stepped from the boardwalk into the frame building and saw a tall man with a rust-colored beard standing behind a counter. "You the ticket agent?" asked Longarm.

"I'm Burke," replied the man, who wore a leather vest and a string tie. "What can I do for you?"

Longarm frowned slightly. "You run this station yourself?"

"When I have to. And for the past week, my regular man's been down with a fever. You need to buy a ticket, mister?" Burke's attitude was brisk and all business, as befitted a co-owner of the stage line.

"The first thing I need is some information." Longarm took both his identification and the photograph of Nora Can-

50

ady from inside his coat. He flipped open the leather folder so that Burke could see the badge, then laid the picture of Nora on the counter. "Ever seen her before?"

Burke looked at the photograph, lines of puzzlement appearing on his forehead. They cleared up almost immediately as he said, "Sure, I remember this woman, Marshal. She came through here sometime in the past couple of days, I'm certain of that."

"She probably came in on the stage from Denver on Tuesday evening."

Burke nodded. "Yes, that sounds right."

"Did she get off the stage? Do you know where she went?"

Instead of answering right away, Burke scratched his beard and said, "Why are you looking for her? Did she do something wrong?"

"That's sort of hard to say right now," Longarm answered truthfully. "What I really want to do is ask her some questions."

"Well, she didn't get off the stage, I remember that now. Or rather, she did, but she got right back on after she came in here and bought a ticket to Tucumcari."

Longarm suppressed a groan. He had really hoped that he would find Nora here in Raton, but it looked as if the chase was going to continue.

"So she was on the stage when it pulled out?"

Burke nodded. "Sure was. I saw her leave."

"What's the quickest way from here to Tucumcari?"

"You could always take the stage," Burke said with a shrug. "Of course, there won't be another one for three days, but . . ."

"Point me to the nearest livery stable," Longarm said grimly.

He went back to the depot and picked up his rifle, carpetbag, and saddle before going in search of the stable. Burke had given him good directions, and Longarm found it with ease.

51

The place was a big barn on a side street, with corrals behind it. Inside the office, Longarm found an old man with bushy white whiskers, sitting behind a desk with his booted feet propped on it. The old man was reading a yellow-backed novel by somebody named Stark, and he put the book down reluctantly when Longarm came in.

"Somethin' I can do you for?"

"I need a couple of good saddle horses," said Longarm.

The old man shifted his feet off the desk and put them on the floor. He sighed again as he placed the dime novel face-down on the desk. "Goin' to swap from one to the other and do some fast travelin', huh?"

"That's the idea, old-timer. Can you help me or not?"

The old man pushed himself to his feet. "Don't get so impatient. Ever'body's turn for the boneyard'll be here soon enough."

"You own this place?"

"Nope. Just the hostler. But I know the horseflesh we got, sonny, don't you worry 'bout that. Come on."

The old man limped out of the office. He led Longarm down the wide aisle in the center of the barn, between the rows of stalls, and stopped in front of one of the enclosures. Inside the stall was a sturdy-looking buckskin mare.

"I know she don't 'pear to be made for speed, but she's got a good pace to her when she gets to goin'," said the old man. "And she gets her strength back quick once you swap out and ride the other hoss for a while."

"All right," said Longarm, who was a pretty good judge of horseflesh himself. "What else have you got?"

"Back here." The old man led the way to another stall, this one in the rear corner of the barn. As he stopped in front of the stall, the horse inside reared up and slammed its hooves angrily against the side wall. Longarm's eyes narrowed as he studied the animal, a rangy, mouse-colored gelding with a darker stripe down its back.

"Sort of touchy, ain't he?"

"Yeah, he's a devil, all right. You want to keep an eye

on him all the time, or he'll reach over and bite a hunk out of you. But once you got a saddle on him, he settles down a mite, and he'll run all day if you ask him to."

Longarm was a little dubious about the dun. It reminded him too much of other rambunctious mounts he'd had in the past. But he nodded again anyway, unwilling to waste any more time. "How much to rent both of them?"

"You aim to go far?"

Longarm didn't know the answer to that. He would go as far as the job took him. He said, "I'll see that they get back to you, don't worry about that."

"If you don't, the fella who owns this place will have the law on you."

"I *am* the law, old-timer," Longarm told him. "U.S. deputy marshal out of Denver."

"You don't say. Well, in that case, I'll give you the special guv'mint rate, which is the exact same as ever'body else pays." The old man named a price. Longarm thought it was a little steep, but he didn't have time for haggling either.

"Done," he said. He hefted the McClellan saddle. "I've got my own saddle, but I'll need blankets and harness."

"I'll fetch 'em from the tack room. You goin' to put the hosses over in the hotel corral till you get ready to leave?"

"I'm not staying at the hotel," Longarm said regretfully. "I'm riding out as soon as I find a store where I can rustle up some supplies."

"Lord, you must be in an all-fired hurry."

"Let's just get these horses ready to travel," suggested Longarm.

Ten minutes later, the price having been paid and the saddle put on the buckskin mare, Longarm rode out of the stable leading the lineback dun. The old man called after him, "If you're lookin' for supplies, go on down the street to Mc-Greevey's. My brother runs it."

"Much obliged," Longarm told him. Now the old man could go back to his dime novel.

Longarm had no trouble finding McGreevey's Emporium,

53

and a short, stout, bald-headed, pink-cheeked man with a high-pitched voice was inside behind the counter. He greeted Longarm by saying, "Howdy, mister. What can I do you for?"

"I'm riding down to Tucumcari. Need supplies for the trip."

"Well, let's see, what'll you need to fix you right up?" The man started gathering up staples, including a small side of bacon and some beans and flour and sugar and salt.

Longarm said, "Don't forget the Arbuckle's, and throw in a couple of airtights with peaches in 'em. And a couple with tomatoes too." As long as he was going to be doing some hard riding, he might as well eat good along the way.

"Yes, sir."

Longarm paid for the supplies and hefted the burlap bags in which the storekeeper placed them. Outside, he tied the bags together and slung them over the back of the dun, which didn't take kindly to being used as a pack animal. The horse showed his disapproval by twisting his head and nipping at Longarm's shoulder. Longarm stepped back quickly, just in time to avoid the slashing teeth.

"Keep it up and I'll introduce that thick skull of yours to the butt of my gun," Longarm muttered. The dun didn't seem impressed by the threat, probably with good reason. If Longarm clouted him over the head, it would probably just break the gun butt.

Longarm swung up into the saddle and followed Raton's main street until it left the settlement and turned into a south-bound road. The trail paralleled the railroad tracks for a couple of miles through a broad valley in the Sangre de Cristos, then forked with one branch continuing to follow the railroad toward Santa Fe while the other veered off to the southeast. That was the stage road to Tucumcari, Longarm knew. He took a firm grip on the reins of the dun that he was leading and heeled the buckskin mare into a fast trot.

The mountains fell away behind him as he rode over a broad, open plain. That prairie stretched a long way, clear over into the Texas Panhandle until it dropped off at the edge of the Cap Rock. The country Longarm was heading into was pretty much lawless; most of the big ranchers in this part of New Mexico Territory had established themselves by rustling raids over the line into Texas. Or if they didn't steal the cattle themselves, they bought rustled herds that had been driven across the border.

Longarm wasn't after rustlers on this trip, though. All he wanted to do was find Nora Canady. That would mean pushing the horses as hard as he dared and riding at night so that he could reach Tucumcari not far behind the stage.

The day grew hotter as it went along. During one of the breaks when he was resting the horses, Longarm took off his coat, vest, and tie and tucked them away inside one of the bags of supplies. He stopped at midday just long enough to build a small fire and fry some bacon. That would have to do for now. Tonight, when he would call a halt for a couple of hours before riding on, he would cook some biscuits as well as more bacon.

During the day, Longarm saw a few riders in the distance, probably cowhands checking on the herds that roamed this vast, unfenced wilderness. None of them paid any attention to him. He didn't encounter any traffic along the road, which was a little surprising. He had thought he might run into a pilgrim or two. Obviously, not too many people traveled between Raton and Tucumcari, and those who did must usually take the stage.

What was a young woman like Nora Canady doing traveling through this country that was pretty much the ass-end of nowhere?

By late afternoon, Longarm's balls were aching again from the seemingly endless hours of riding. He was determined to push on as long as he could stand it, however, and a little later, as the sun sank beneath the western horizon and dusk began to gather, he spotted lights twinkling up ahead in the distance. Had to be a settlement, he decided. There were too many lights for it to be a ranch headquarters.

Longarm's brain commenced to waging war with itself. After a long day in the saddle, it would do his injured privates a world of good to spend the night in a regular bed. There might be a hotel in that settlement, even if it wasn't fancy. On the other hand, he had planned to stop for just a couple of hours, eat some supper and grab a little sleep, then resume his pursuit of Nora Canady. Save some time or take it easy on his aching balls? That was the question, thought Longarm, and at this moment, it seemed every bit as profound a dilemma as anything that fella Hamlet had chewed the scenery over in that old play.

Well, there was bound to be a saloon in that town, he told himself. He'd have a drink first and then decide what to do.

But instead, he had walked into more trouble, because that kid with the Dragoon Colt had taken one look at him and pulled that hogleg, and then Longarm had been forced to kill him, and now Longarm found himself standing at the bar in this nameless saloon in a little New Mexico town that was evidently called Ashcroft.

"A bride?" repeated the bartender, snapping Longarm's thoughts back to the present. "Did you say you're looking for a bride, mister?"

Longarm shook his head. "It's a long story," he said.

"Well, I don't know that there's anybody here in town you'd actually want to marry, but there's a gal or two who'd be glad to *pretend* to be your wife for an hour or so. Of course, it'd cost you."

Longarm smiled faintly. "So does getting hitched, from what I've heard." He tossed back the rest of his drink. A scraping sound made him look around. A couple of men were dragging the body of the kid out of the saloon. The sound came from his boot heels dragging along the floorboards. They went out, and the bat-wings flapped back and forth for a few seconds as if waving farewell to the dead man.

"The stage that runs from Raton to Tucumcari comes

through here, doesn't it?'' Longarm asked the bartender.

"Sure does. You've missed it for this week, though. It came through day before yesterday, won't be another one for three days.''

Longarm nodded. Even riding hard all day, he hadn't managed to shave much off the lead that Nora had on him. Well, that decided things, he told himself. He would push on and ride several hours tonight.

He rattled a coin on the bar and said, "Much obliged. Sorry about getting blood on the floor.''

The bartender shrugged. "You didn't have much choice in the matter. Billy was just too damned foolish to live, I reckon.''

Longarm couldn't argue with that, although it had been his experience that most folks, at one time or another, were too foolish to live, including himself. Some were just luckier than others.

He pushed through the bat-wings and stepped out onto Ashcroft's rickety boardwalk. The town had just one street, and the businesses were all lined up along one side of it. There were a few shacks on the other side of the street, all of them just dark hulks at this time of night. Folks turned in early around here. The saloon, a small cafe, and the hotel down the street were the only places still showing lights. Longarm turned toward the cafe. He had to eat anyway before he pushed on. Might as well take a break from his own cooking and make his supplies last longer.

He had only gone a couple of steps when flame lanced from a gun muzzle across the street and something sang wickedly past his ear.

Chapter 8

The glass in the saloon's front window shattered in a million pieces as Longarm flung himself forward. He landed hard on the boardwalk, the Colt already in his hand as he sprawled out. He knew all too well what had hummed past his ear. Too many bullets had come his way for him not to recognize their song.

He had seen the muzzle flash from the corner of his eye. It had come from one of the shacks across the street. He triggered a pair of shots in that direction, then scrambled to his feet and ran a couple of steps to a water trough, which was the nearest good cover. As he bellied down behind the trough, the rifle across the street blasted again and a slug thudded into the thick wood. From the sound of the shots, the man gunning for him was using a Spencer carbine, Longarm decided. That meant he probably had five shots left before he would need to reload. That was three more than Longarm had.

Longarm had an ally, though. The bartender came bursting out through the bat-wings carrying an old Sharps. "Where's the son of a bitch who shot out my window?" he bellowed.

"Get down!" Longarm called to him. "He's over there across the street!"

The fella with the Spencer had already cut loose at the

bartender, though. The bullet missed narrowly and smacked into the wall next to the door of the saloon. The bartender whipped the Sharps to his shoulder and pulled the trigger of the buffalo gun. It boomed like a cannon and threw a slug damned near as big, and the recoil knocked the bartender back a step. At the same time, Longarm fired again toward the spot where he thought the rifleman was.

That was enough for the bushwhacker. Longarm caught a glimpse of him in the moonlight as he ducked back around the corner of the shack. The man was tall and lean and wore a broad-brimmed hat and a long duster. A second later, Longarm heard rapid hoofbeats.

The bartender came down the boardwalk toward Longarm. "You all right, Marshal?" he asked.

"Yeah," Longarm replied as he pushed himself to his feet. The hoofbeats had just about faded away already. "That fella's in a hurry."

"Damn good thing for him too," growled the bartender. "I had the glass for that window freighted all the way out here from St. Louis. It was the only window that big between Amarillo and Santa Fe. Do you know how much it's going to cost to replace it?"

"Wouldn't have any idea."

"Was that bastard shooting at you?"

"I reckon so," said Longarm. "It was my head his first shot nearly took off. I'm sorry about your window, by the way." He shook his head ruefully. "Next time somebody ambushes me, I'll tell 'em to be more careful where they're aiming."

"Well, I reckon it ain't your fault, Marshal." The bartender clapped a hand on Longarm's shoulder. "Come on back inside and have a drink on me. Say, you think we winged that fella?"

Longarm shook his head. "He was moving mighty spry when he lit a shuck out of here. Didn't look hurt to me."

"Me neither, more's the pity." The bartender paused, then asked, "Do folks shoot at you like that all the time?"

"Not *all* the time," Longarm said dryly. "But too often for my tastes."

Well, the murder attempts were up to four now, Longarm thought as he rode out of Ashcroft an hour later: two in Denver by the man named Ross; once on the train by the deceptively innocent-looking Emily Toplin; and now these shots out of the darkness from an unseen, unknown stranger.

Could the rifleman back in Ashcroft have been Badger Bob McGurk? Longarm asked himself as he chewed on an unlit cheroot. After a moment, he shook his head. The bushwhacker had been too tall to be McGurk, unless ol' Bob had grown half a foot while he was in prison. McGurk wasn't big, just mean and deadly. That was one reason he'd picked up the nickname Badger, that and his ugly, pointed face and the white streak in his dark hair. He just looked like a badger, Longarm recalled, and had the disposition of one as well.

Longarm could have written off the attempts on his life by Ross as being connected to McGurk's grudge against him, since the men had been cell mates. But for the life of him, he couldn't see a woman like Emily Toplin being involved with somebody like McGurk. And he couldn't tie that tall stranger in with McGurk either. Somebody else wanted him dead. Maybe Ross had been working for whoever had sent Emily and the fella with the Spencer after him. Longarm recalled Billy Vail saying that Ross had been in trouble already since being released from prison. The law even suspected that Ross had killed a couple of folks. It could have been pure coincidence that somebody hired him to put a bullet in Longarm. Ross might not have even known that McGurk had busted out of prison.

Lord, it was all too complicated, Longarm told himself as he rode along on the dun, having switched the saddle from the buckskin before leaving Ashcroft. The moonlight made it easy to follow the stage road, and he felt himself getting sleepy. But he could push on for a while longer before rolling in his soogans for a couple of hours of sleep.

The thing of it was, the only case he was working on at the moment was the disappearance of Nora Canady. And only a few people knew he was looking for the young woman, chief among them being Billy Vail, Bryce Canady, and Jonas Palmer. Longarm would trust Vail with his life. Canady and Palmer were a different story. Either of them could have sent the killers after Longarm.

But why would they do that? Both men had seemed desperate for him to find Nora and bring her back to Denver.

Longarm scrubbed a hand over his face and yawned. Maybe the answer to that question, like the answers to all the other questions, lay with Miss Nora Canady.

He was going to have a long talk with that young lady when he finally caught up with her.

Nobody tried to kill him the rest of the night, which meant it was pretty successful, Longarm thought the next morning. He had ridden until well after midnight before making a cold camp, then was up before the sun and on the trail again after a quick breakfast. He wished he had a bottle of rye so that he could have added a dollop to his coffee, but the Arbuckle's served as a pretty good eye-opener by itself.

Late in the day, he crossed the Canadian River, which meant that he wasn't too far from Tucumcari. The town was bigger than Ashcroft, he knew, but still not what anybody would consider a city. He had his doubts that Nora would still be there, but he supposed it couldn't hurt to hope.

Longarm rode into town a little after dusk. Several people were still on the street, so he looked them over closely. None of them were Nora Canady, nor did he catch sight of a tall man in a broad-brimmed hat and long duster. When he spotted a sign on a small frame building that read SHERIFF'S OFFICE, he veered the buckskin toward it.

When he had the two horses tied up at the hitch rack, he stepped up onto the boardwalk and crossed to the door of the sheriff's office. Without knocking, he went inside and found a medium-sized man with dark hair standing beside a potbellied stove and pouring coffee from a battered old pot into a chipped china cup. The man finished his task, set the pot back on the stove, and laid aside the piece of leather he had used to grip the handle, then turned to Longarm with a nod. "Evening," he said. "Can I help you?"

"You the law hereabouts?" asked Longarm.

"That's right. I'm Sheriff Holmes."

"Name's Custis Long, U.S. deputy marshal out of Denver."

Holding his coffee cup in his left hand, Holmes stepped forward and extended his right. "Glad to meet you, Marshal," he said as he shook hands with Longarm. "I take it your business has brought you here to Tucumcari?"

"That's right." Longarm decided Holmes looked like an honest man, so he went on. "I'm looking for a young woman who disappeared from Denver. Have you seen her?" He took the photograph from his pocket and showed it to Holmes.

The local lawman studied it, a frown creasing his forehead as he did so. "Something about her seems familiar," he said, "but I can't quite place her...."

"Did you happen to see the stage from Raton come in a couple of days ago?"

Holmes snapped his fingers. "That's it! She was on the stage."

"You're sure?"

"I'm certain," Holmes said with a nod. "I make it my business to watch the stage come in every time I can, so I can keep track of any strangers getting off. Tucumcari can be a pretty rough place sometimes, so I try to stay one step ahead of trouble when I can." Holmes sipped from the cup of coffee.

Longarm noted the width of the sheriff's shoulders and the easy grace with which he moved, and decided that the man's mild appearance was deceiving. He imagined Holmes could be every bit as rough as anybody else in Tucumcari when he had to.

"You wouldn't happen to know where this young lady

went when she got off the stage, would you?'' he asked.

Holmes shook his head. ''I didn't say she got off the stage. Well, actually, she did, but only to go into the station for a few minutes. Then she got back on the coach, and she was in it when it rolled out of here a few minutes later.''

Longarm's jaw tightened, and he couldn't stop himself from saying a clipped, ''Damn.''

Holmes studied him shrewdly. ''I reckon you must've been hoping you'd catch up to her here.''

''That would have been the easiest,'' admitted Longarm. ''Looks like I've still got some riding to do.''

''You say this young woman disappeared from Denver. She must've done it on her own, because she sure didn't look like anybody was forcing her to do anything.''

Longarm shrugged. ''Right now, I'm not over sure of anything where this case is concerned.''

''Is she a criminal?''

''Not that I know of,'' Longarm answered honestly. ''I just want to catch up to her and ask her some questions.''

''I've got one for you, Marshal. How about a cup of coffee? You look like you could use it.''

Longarm grinned tiredly. ''I reckon I could at that. Much obliged.''

When Holmes had poured the coffee for him, Longarm sat down on an old divan with busted springs and sipped the strong, black brew. Holmes settled down behind the desk. He was obviously curious about Longarm's assignment, but he was reluctant to pry into another star packer's business.

''Where does the stage road go from here?'' Longarm asked.

''Down along the border between New Mexico and Texas, past the Guadalupes, then into the Davis Mountains and on to the Big Bend.''

''In other words, a whole heap of nothing.''

Holmes chuckled. ''Yep, that's about right. But it connects with the Butterfield line there in West Texas, so folks can get just about anywhere from there.''

In other words, Nora was still ahead of Longarm, and there was no way of knowing which direction she would go next.

"Well, I'm obliged for the coffee and the information," said Longarm after he had drained the last of the scalding liquid from the cup. "I'll grab a bite to eat and then push on."

Holmes frowned. "No offense, Marshal, but you already look like you've been rode hard and put up wet. And you were limping a little when you came in here. You might ought to put up at the hotel and get a good night's sleep."

Longarm shook his head. "Afraid I don't have time for that, no matter how good it sounds. I've got to catch up to that stagecoach."

"Because that's the job."

"Because that's the job," agreed Longarm.

Holmes nodded, clearly understanding what Longarm meant. "All right then. Good luck to you." He stood up and shook hands again.

Longarm paused before leaving the office and asked, "Say, you haven't seen a stranger in town today, have you? Tall, slender gent with a big hat and a long coat?"

"Can't say as I have."

"What about a gal about this tall?" Longarm held out a hand to approximate Emily Toplin's height. "Young, brown hair, pretty in the sort of way you'd want a gal to be if you were taking her to meet your mama." And damned cold-blooded to boot, he thought, but kept that to himself.

Again Holmes shook his head. "Doesn't sound like anybody I know right off hand. There aren't that many pretty young girls in this town. You know how it is out here on the frontier."

Longarm nodded. Once you got out of the big cities, young, attractive women were always in short supply. That was why the soiled doves in small towns were usually long in the tooth—when they had any teeth left at all.

He hadn't really expected Emily Toplin to come after him, Longarm mused as he left the sheriff's office. But he supposed it was possible. As for the bushwhacker who had tried for him in Ashcroft, that gent could be just about anywhere. And knowing that made Longarm a mite tense as he took his horses to a livery stable for food and water and a rub-down, then walked along Tucumcari's main street in search of a hash house where he could grab a surrounding before riding out again.

No gunfire came out of the shadows. Longarm had a steak fried up by a Chinaman in a narrow little cafe and topped off with a mound of fried potatoes. He reclaimed the horses from the stable, flipped a coin to the bandy-legged hostler who had cared for them, then rode out of Tucumcari, once again following the stage road by the light of the stars and the newly risen moon.

He wasn't sure how much of a lead the stagecoach still had on him, or how far Nora Canady intended to ride it, or why people had been trying to kill him. He wasn't sure of much of anything except that he was tired and his balls still hurt some. But as he rode south that night, and the next day, and the night and day after that, he knew that he was getting farther and farther away from anywhere that a young woman such as Nora would normally want to be. Whatever had caused her to leave Denver must have been pretty urgent, especially since it had kept her running for such a long way.

Longarm didn't sleep for more than a couple of hours at a time, and then only when he was so tired he found himself dozing off in the saddle. He imagined the vast prairie over which he rode as a map on brown parchment, and he could see his progress marked on it as a dotted line, stretching ever southward toward Texas. Surely, the way he was pushing himself, sooner or later he would catch up to that stagecoach.

He stopped at every way station and asked about Nora, just to make certain she hadn't gotten off at one of them. The hostlers who ran the stations remembered her, all right— men stuck out in the middle of nowhere tended to remember the infrequent pretty girl they encountered—but all of them told Longarm that Nora had moved on with the stage, not doing any more than getting out of the coach for a few minutes to stretch her legs.

A range of mountains began to loom to the west. Longarm recognized them as the Sacramentos. When those peaks petered out, they were soon replaced by the Guadalupes, which were dominated by Guadalupe Peak itself and a particularly rugged-looking mountain known as El Capitan that was almost as tall. When Longarm saw them off to his right, he knew he had crossed the border. He was in Texas now.

But the plains around him didn't change any. They were still flat, virtually treeless except for a few scrubby mesquites, and covered with short but hardy grass that grew from the sandy soil. This was poor country for ranching, but on the other hand, that was about all it was good for. It just took a lot of range to support very many cows.

The sun was overhead, blazing down mercilessly at midday, when Longarm stopped at a way station and asked his usual questions about Nora and the coach that was carrying her.

"Yes, sir, she was here," the boy who was running the place told him. He was no more than seventeen, sunburned and carrot-topped. "A mighty pretty lady. She ate breakfast here, though I wished I'd had somethin' better to offer her than beans."

Longarm was standing beside the horses while they drank from the station's trough. "She ate breakfast, you say. Was that yesterday morning?"

"Naw, this mornin'."

Longarm was stretching, trying to ease sore back muscles. He stiffened again in surprise at what the young hostler had said. "Are you sure of that?" Just the day before, he had still been more than twenty-four hours behind the coach.

"Yep. The coach was way behind schedule. Busted an axle up north of here, the jehu said, and he like to never got it fixed good enough to drive. Had to limp on in here, and the passengers spent the night whilst the driver and me got that axle replaced. The one we put on there had a crack in it too, but it wasn't busted clear through. Wrapped some tin around it, so it ought to hold up all right, as long as the driver don't take it too fast.'' The talkative youngster shook his head. ''Sure goin' to play hell with the schedule, though.''

Longarm nodded. He had finally had some good luck. Impatiently, he waited for the water in the trough to settle after the horses got through drinking, then filled his canteens. ''Much obliged for the water . . . and the information.''

''You bet. Come back any time, mister.''

Not unless he had to, thought Longarm. This was mighty unappealing country.

But for the first time in several days, he felt some excitement because he was closing in on his quarry, and that seemed to communicate itself to the dun. The horse stepped along lively, and so did the buckskin as Longarm led it. With any luck, he might come up on the stagecoach tomorrow, or possibly even today.

The thought that he might have some answers before the sun went down made him lean forward a little in anticipation.

The heat got worse—but what else could you expect from West Texas in the summertime? Longarm mopped sweat from his face, gave the horses a short rest whenever he could, and pushed on through the afternoon. He stopped at another way station and found that the stage, traveling slowly as the redheaded youngster had said that it would have to, was only about an hour ahead of him now. His horses were getting tired, but Longarm urged them on and they responded.

The terrain took on a little more of a rolling nature. From the top of one of the little hills, Longarm spotted dust rising ahead of him. A thrill shot through him. More than likely, that dust was being kicked up by the hooves of the team and the wheels of the coach. He flapped the reins and clucked to the dun to prod it into a faster gait, and although the horse turned its head enough to give him a walleyed look, it broke into a run.

Longarm kept an eye on the dust rising into the brassy

blue sky ahead of him. The distance between him and it was steadily closing, when suddenly the dust cloud disappeared. The coach must have stopped moving. If that was the case, the hot Texas wind would quickly dissipate the dust. Maybe the stagecoach had reached another way station and halted for a change of teams.

But that wasn't the case, Longarm saw as he topped the crest of another small rise and looked out across a mesquite-dotted flat in front of him. He reined in and narrowed his eyes in a squint, wishing that he had a pair of field glasses. Even without such an aid, he could see that the stagecoach had stopped in the middle of nowhere. There was no way station, no settlement, no signs of civilization at all. Only the coach, sitting there in the road.

And the men on horseback sitting around it, pointing guns at the driver, who had his hands in the air over his head.

Longarm said, "Oh, *hell*!"

The stagecoach carrying Nora Canady was being held up by outlaws.

Chapter 9

Even as that realization hit him, Longarm dropped the reins of the buckskin, jammed his heels into the flanks of the dun, and grabbed the stock of his Winchester as the horse lunged forward in a gallop.

Chances were, the outlaws would just steal the mail pouch, rob the passengers of any valuables, and ride off. But you could never tell what might happen in such a tense situation. One of the passengers might foolishly decide to fight back, or the driver could try to make a play, or one of the owlhoots might start shooting just for the hell of it. . . . The important thing was, Nora could be in danger.

He was too far away to have an effect on the outcome of the robbery, Longarm realized sickly. The outlaws' horses were already milling around, as if the gang was getting ready to ride off. Longarm saw several figures standing beside the coach, one of them a woman. Suddenly, one of the outlaws spurred his horse closer to her and bent over. Longarm was too far away to hear the scream she must have let out as the desperado wrapped his arm around her and jerked her off her feet, but the terrified cry echoed in his imagination. The hat the woman was wearing came off as the outlaw swung her onto the horse in front of him. Late afternoon sunlight flashed on long, honey-blond hair as it spilled free.

Longarm turned the air around his head blue with curses as he rode desperately toward the scene of the holdup. The outlaws were grabbing Nora, most likely to take her with them as a hostage. She was actually being kidnapped this time.

Longarm yanked the dun to a stop and brought the Winchester to his shoulder. He fired, deliberately aiming wide of the stagecoach and the men on horseback around it. He couldn't risk trying to shoot any of the outlaws, not while Nora was their prisoner and might get hit by a stray slug, but maybe he could spook the man who was holding her and give her a chance to slip away.

That didn't prove to be the case. The outlaws wheeled their horses and broke into a gallop that carried them away from the stage road to the east. Longarm slid the rifle back into its sheath. There was no point in throwing lead after them, not at this range. He heeled the dun into motion again.

Instead of following the outlaws directly, he rode on to the stopped stagecoach instead. It had occurred to him that maybe the woman the owlhoots had snatched hadn't been Nora. There could have been more than one woman on the coach, although he hadn't heard anything about that at any of the stations where he had stopped. He had to be sure, though, before he took off after the outlaws.

The middle-aged driver was waiting, along with three passengers, all men, when Longarm rode up. "Wish you'd happened along a mite sooner, mister," the driver called up to him. "You might've spooked those bastards 'fore they cleaned us out."

Two of the passengers appeared to be salesmen, while the third had the look of a cattleman. Longarm said to them, "That woman who was carried off, do any of you know her name?"

The question took them by surprise, but the rancher said, "I believe she told us her name was Cassidy."

"That's right," added one of the drummers. "Miss Nora Cassidy."

The other drummer said, "She told us she was going down to Fort Davis to meet her fiancé, a lieutenant who's posted there."

"You goin' after those boys, mister?" asked the driver.

Longarm nodded grimly. "I intend to get that woman back."

"By God, I'll go with you!" exclaimed the rancher. He nodded toward the buckskin, which had trotted up following Longarm and the dun. "That is, if you'll loan me a horse."

Longarm hesitated. The cattleman was past his prime, as evidenced by his white hair and mustache and the thickness of his waist. But his eyes flashed with outrage at the idea of a woman being kidnapped or mistreated in any way, and his rough, big-knuckled hands showed the signs of a lifetime of hard work. If he had established a ranch anywhere out here in West Texas, chances were he still had a lot of bark on his hide despite his age.

"All right," Longarm said, coming to a decision. He might need someone to back his play when he caught up to the bandits. "I don't have an extra saddle, though."

"Don't matter. Mine's in the boot." The rancher started toward the rear of the coach, only to pause and extend a hand up to Longarm. "Name's Walt Gibson."

"Custis Long," Longarm told him as he shook hands. He didn't take the time to explain that he was a United States marshal.

While Gibson was getting his saddle from the coach's boot, Longarm untied the two bags of supplies from each other, then tied one onto the horn of his saddle. Gibson would carry the other one on the buckskin.

"What's the nearest town?" Longarm asked the driver.

"That'd be Monahans. It's our next stop, in fact."

"Is there any law there?"

"County sheriff."

Longarm nodded. "Good. Tell him what happened here, and that Gibson and I have gone after those outlaws. You happen to know who those fellas were?"

"Couldn't see their faces," said the jehu. "They had bandannas pulled up over their mouths. But I'd be willing to bet it was the Heck Wallace gang."

"Sounds like a bunch that's well known in these parts."

One of the drummers said, "You haven't heard of the Wallace gang, mister?"

"I ain't from around here," Longarm said dryly.

"They've been holding up stagecoaches and robbing banks from Big Springs to El Paso for the past six months," the driver said. "I was warned to be on the lookout for 'em. They rode up out of a dry wash right over yonder, though, so I didn't even have time to whip up the team 'fore they had us surrounded."

"I'm ready to ride," Gibson announced. He swung up into the saddle on the back of the buckskin.

Longarm nodded. "Remember to tell the sheriff in Monahans what happened," he told the driver.

"Don't worry about that, Mr. Long. His office is goin' to be my first stop!"

Longarm and Gibson trotted their mounts away from the stage road, heading east the way the outlaws had done. When Longarm glanced behind them, he saw that the coach had gotten underway and was rolling south again.

"I appreciate you coming along, Gibson," he told the rancher. "Looked like there were seven or eight men in that gang. Hefty odds for only one man to go up against."

"Yep, now it's only four to one," Gibson said with a grin. Longarm couldn't help but chuckle at the anticipation he heard in the cattleman's voice. Gibson was obviously spoiling for some action.

"You have a spread around here somewhere?" Longarm asked.

Gibson nodded. "Down by San Solomon Springs, about fifty miles southwest of here. My foreman was going to meet me with some horses in Monahans. I took a herd up into New Mexico Territory and sold it, decided to come back on the stage instead of riding back with my cowhands." He grunted. "Bad mistake. I was cut out for a saddle, not no bouncin', dust-choked contraption like that stagecoach."

Longarm's liking for the man grew. He had never been overly fond of riding a stagecoach either. "You talk much to Miss Cassidy while you were traveling together?" he asked. It didn't surprise him that Nora had used a phony name. Too many people had heard of Bryce Canady and might connect her with him if she used her real name. That was more proof—as if he'd needed it—that leaving Denver had been Nora's own idea. She was running away and evidently didn't want to go back.

But he was sure she didn't want to be in the hands of a bunch of outlaws either.

"No, she was pretty quiet, kept to herself," Gibson said. "Pleasant enough, just not the sort to talk much. We all respected that, of course." The rancher's face and voice hardened. "Those bastards had best not harm her. If they do, every man west of the Brazos will want to hunt them down and string them up like the skunks they are."

"I reckon they know that too," said Longarm. That knowledge was the hole card he was counting on. The outlaws might use Nora as a hostage or even hold her for ransom, but there was a good chance they wouldn't molest her. Mistreating a decent woman was something that just wasn't tolerated on the frontier.

The riders Longarm and Gibson were trailing had left tracks that were plain to see. Evidently, they weren't worried about pursuit. Longarm thought about that for a minute, recalled some things about West Texas geography he had learned on previous visits to the Lone Star State, then said, "We're heading toward those damned sand hills, aren't we?"

"I'm afraid so," said Gibson. "Rumor has it that Wallace has a hideout somewhere in there." He shook his head. "It's hellish country, I know that."

So did Longarm. Mile after mile of sand dunes that constantly shifted under the push of winds that never stopped blowing. The almost-white sand reflected the sun and the heat until riding through the dunes was like traveling through a blast furnace. And the soft sand sank under the hooves of horses and the feet of men alike, so that walking through it was even worse than slogging through mud. Over the years, a lot of people had tried to cross those sand hills. The bones of many of them were still bleaching in the West Texas sun. An entire wagon train had even disappeared in there, Longarm recalled. The sands seemed to have swallowed it whole, wagons, mules, and dozens of immigrants all vanishing.

"There's water in there, if you know where to look," Gibson went on. "The Comanches used to hole up in there. They never had any trouble finding water."

"What about you?" asked Longarm. "Ever been across the sand hills?"

The cattleman shook his head. "Nope. Been on the edges, maybe a mile or so into them, but that's all. That was enough for me. It's a good seventy miles across there from west to east, and God knows how far they stretch to the north. Clear up into New Mexico, I reckon."

"And if Wallace and his bunch get there before us, it'll be hard to track them. The wind will wipe out any sign in an hour or two."

"That's right. That's why I'm hopin' we'll catch up to 'em before they get to the sand."

Longarm hoped so, too. Nora Canady's safety—her very life—might depend on it.

And there was nightfall to contend with too. The sun was already low in the western sky behind them. The trail would be harder to follow once it got dark. Longarm wasn't the sort to give in to despair, but if he had been, he might be feeling it now. To have tracked Nora so far and come so close to her, only to have her snatched away from him like this . . .

He pushed that thought out of his mind and told himself to concentrate on the job at hand.

A few minutes later, he and Gibson both saw dust ahead of them at the same time. The rancher pointed it out and said, "Got to be them."

Longarm leaned forward in the saddle. "Yeah. Come on."

Both men heeled their horses into a run. The dun was getting tired, Longarm could feel that, but he hoped the horse had the stamina to stand up under the strain a while longer.

The riders who were kicking up dust in front of them seemed to be moving along at a pretty good clip, but nothing like the pace Longarm and Gibson set for themselves. The two pursuers rapidly closed the distance between themselves and the outlaws. They came in sight of their quarry just as the bandits were about to enter a wide, dry wash between two hills littered with boulders.

Longarm reined in sharply as he saw a glint of light from behind one of those rocks. Sunlight was reflecting off something hidden back there, and there was only one thing it was likely to be.

"Look!" Longarm's hand shot out and gripped Gibson's arm. "They're riding into some sort of ambush."

Gibson's deep-set eyes, surrounded by wrinkles caused by years of squinting into the sun, did just that once again. He said, "Damned if you're not right. There are men hidin' behind those rocks, and Wallace is so damned confident he's ridin' right into their sights!"

Longarm's brain worked furiously. He knew that the Wallace gang had been raising hell in these parts for quite a while, and it was entirely possible that was a sheriff's posse or a troop of Rangers concealed there on the hills, having laid this trap for the outlaws without even knowing that the gang had just held up a stagecoach. The men waiting in ambush couldn't possibly know about Nora Canady being kidnapped either. The stage hadn't even had time to reach Monahans yet.

But surely they would see her and realize she was a

woman. Surely they would hold their fire. . . .

Because if they didn't, once the gang was in that wash, they would be easy targets for the riflemen concealed on the hillsides. The whole bunch might be cut down like a field of wheat before the scythe.

With only the glimmerings of a plan beginning to form in his head, Longarm reached for his Winchester.

"What're you doin'?" asked Gibson.

"Can't let that ambush go ahead," said Longarm. "A stray bullet might hit the girl."

"Yeah, but you can't interfere—"

"The hell I can't," said Longarm as he brought the Winchester to his shoulder and began firing as fast as he could work the lever and jack fresh cartridges into the chamber.

He aimed high, sending the slugs well over the heads of the outlaws and into the dry wash in front of them. The sharp *crack!-crack!-crack!* of the rifle made the outlaws jerk their horses to a halt and whirl around to see where the shots were coming from. They stopped short of the wash that would have been their death trap.

Longarm's shots had another effect. Waiting to ambush somebody usually wound a man pretty tightly, and a couple of the posse members fired instinctively when they heard the rattle of shots. That was all the warning Wallace and his men needed. They spurred furiously away from the wash.

Gibson leaned over and grabbed the barrel of Longarm's Winchester, forcing the rifle down. "Damn you!" the cattleman yelled. "You warned them!"

Now that the ambush was ruined, all the men who were hidden on the hills opened fire, but it was too late. Instead of being trapped in the wash, the outlaws were running free, spreading out and throwing a few shots of their own back at the hills. That was just what Longarm had hoped would happen.

He jerked his rifle out of Gibson's grasp. "You don't know everything that's going on here, Walt," he snapped. "I wish you'd trust me on this—"

"Trust, hell! You're no better'n an owlhoot yourself!" Gibson clawed at the butt of the revolver holstered at his hip.

Longarm lashed out with the butt of the Winchester, slamming it into Gibson's jaw and knocking the rancher from the saddle. His gun went flying from its holster and landed on the sandy ground several feet away. Longarm swung down quickly from his own saddle and kicked the gun farther away.

"Sorry, Walt," he said, though Gibson was stunned and probably didn't understand the words. "Hope I can explain all this to you someday." Longarm jerked the bag of supplies loose from the saddlehorn. "I'll leave you the buckskin. I wouldn't set a man afoot out here."

He mounted up again and wheeled the dun around. The outlaws had split up to a certain extent, but most of them were galloping off to the north, toward a couple of buttes that jutted up from the plains. Longarm went after them.

He hoped that Walt Gibson was all right. The rancher hadn't given him much choice. To Gibson's eyes, it had appeared that Longarm was trying to help the outlaws.

And when you got right down to it, that was true. He hadn't wanted them to ride into that ambush. Nora might have gotten hurt. Besides, this might be a way for Longarm to solve the other problems that were facing him.

He was going to turn outlaw.

Chapter 10

Longarm rode hard, knowing that he was calling on the dun for the last reserves of its strength. His only advantage was that he was pursuing the outlaws from an angle now, and he was soon able to cut down the gap between them. He glanced over his left shoulder and saw that the sun wasn't very far above the horizon. It would be dark in an hour or so, and Longarm wanted to join up with the gang before then.

A look in the other direction showed him dust hanging in the air. That would be coming from the posse, which was now pursuing the gang on horseback. But the outlaws had a good lead, and Longarm didn't think the lawmen would catch up before Wallace's bunch reached the edge of the sand hills.

Longarm was within a few hundred yards of the nearest outlaws now, riding almost parallel with them. He took off his hat and waved it in the air to get their attention. As long as he was doing that, they would know that he wasn't trying to shoot at them. He veered the dun and came closer to the riders. A few minutes later, he was close enough to get a good look at them—and vice versa. With his clothes covered by trail dust and a few days' worth of beard stubble on his face, he hoped he looked as disreputable as he felt right now.

He clapped his hat back on his head and spurred on to join the outlaws.

"Howdy!" he called over the pounding of hoofbeats as he came up alongside the riders. None of them had Nora Canady with them, he saw, but this was where he had to start.

"Who the hell are you?" shouted one of the men. All of them were holding guns, and Longarm knew that if he played this wrong, he might easily wind up being riddled with bullets.

"Name's Parker!" he called back, using, as he often did, his own middle name as an alias. "I'm the fella who tipped you off to that ambush back there at the wash!"

"Much obliged!" said one of the other men. "But why'd you do that?"

Longarm grinned wolfishly. "Never did like to see anybody shot down like a dog! Besides, you're the Wallace bunch, ain't you?"

"What if we are?" demanded the first man.

"I've been looking to join up with you boys! Heard a lot about you!"

The riders slowed their horses to a trot and regarded Longarm intently. He saw suspicion in their eyes. No man who was on the dodge lived very long by being trusting. After a moment, one of the outlaws said, "You're a wanted man yourself, are you?"

Longarm nodded. "Damn right. I was riding with the Pollard gang, up Wyoming way, until lately." He happened to know that Lem Pollard and most of the men who had been riding with him had been either killed or captured in a botched bank robbery in Cheyenne a few weeks earlier. It was entirely plausible that he could have been one of the few survivors to get away.

"You were part of that bank job in Cheyenne?" asked one of the men.

"Yep. Some damn law dog's bullet like to parted my hair for me too."

"Heard it was quite a fight."

"That it was," Longarm said solemnly. "I was lucky to get out with a whole hide. Been riding south ever since. Heard about the hell you boys've been raising down here in Texas while I was up in Tucumcari, and I said to myself, that's the bunch you ought to join up with, old son." He paused, then, added, "You are the Wallace bunch, aren't you?"

The outlaws ignored his question, and one of them barked a question instead. "How'd you know about that ambush?"

"Pure luck. I saw your dust and was trying to catch up to you when I spotted the sun shining on a rifle barrel up on that slope. Didn't take long then to see where those bastards were hiding. They'd started moving out a little to get a better shot at you when you rode into that wash. What were they, sheriff's deputies or Rangers?"

"Don't know. But we've heard that Major Jones sent a whole troop of Rangers out here from Austin just to run us down."

Longarm let out a whistle of admiration. "You fellas must be ring-tailed wonders, to get a whole troop of Rangers after you!"

His reaction concealed what he was really feeling, which was a considerable amount of worry. Having a bunch of Rangers roaming around the countryside would just make things that much more complicated. He hoped he could get Nora away from the outlaws quickly. If he could accomplish that, then the Rangers could have the Wallace bunch, with his blessings.

His words of praise were effective. The outlaws stuck their chests out and looked satisfied with themselves. "I reckon we've got quite a rep, all right," one of them said. He leaned over slightly in the saddle and extended a hand to Longarm. "I'm called Van Horn."

Longarm shook hands, and the other outlaws introduced themselves as Dutchy, Graydon, and Funderburk. Van Horn seemed to be in command of this little bunch, so it was to him that Longarm directed what was apparently a casual question.

"I reckon you boys plan to rendezvous wherever you've been holing up back in the sand hills?"

"That's the plan," said Van Horn.

"I hope you can see your way clear to taking me with you, since I lent you a hand back there where you were almost ambushed."

Van Horn considered for a moment, then nodded. "We'll take you to the hideout, all right," he said. "But that's no guarantee you'll ever get out of there alive. That'll be up to Heck."

"Heck Wallace?"

"That's right. He'll decide if you're all right and can ride with us . . . or if you're a damned lying lawman, in which case I wouldn't give you a plugged nickel for your chances of living very long, mister."

"Me, a lawman?" Longarm hooted with laughter. "Just lead the way, Van Horn. I reckon when he hears what I did for you boys, Mr. Heck Wallace is going to be mighty glad to see me!"

The sand hills started gradually. There were narrow stretches where sand had collected in the low places between rises. Longarm and his companions crossed several of those stretches, which were divided by broader bands of ground that were a mixture of sand, rock, and tough grass and mesquite trees. But as they swung further east and rode on, the sand became more and more prevalent, and then finally, as they topped a rise, Longarm saw the dunes take over the landscape completely, white mounds that rolled away to the horizon like waves in a stormy sea.

And those dunes moved like waves too, Longarm knew, only a lot slower. But they were always in motion, drifting along before the wind so that in a week's time their contours might change completely. Sometimes, when the wind blew harder, the dunes shifted even faster. Old-timers called them the walking hills, and it was an apt description.

As the outlaws entered the dunes, they stuck to the low places, where the sand was packed harder and made easier going for the horses. Now that dusk was settling down, the hills lost some of their brilliance and took on a gloomy air instead, rising sometimes seventy or eighty feet above the men riding through them and bulking darkly as if they were about to crash down on the puny humans who dared to invade them.

The eerie landscape wasn't completely barren. Dwarf oaks grew in many of the low places, rarely reaching a height of more than three or four feet. Longarm knew that their roots extended much farther under the ground so that they could suck up as much life-giving moisture as possible. He commented on that to Van Horn, who nodded and said, "Yeah, those are shin oaks. The Comanches used 'em to find water when they'd run off in here after their raids on the settlements. Dig down around the roots of those shin oaks and you'll hit water, sure as shootin'. Drink your fill, put the sand back in the hole, and nobody would ever know there was a water hole where you'd been. Heck knows, though. He knows every place in this whole godforsaken desert where a man can find water."

"Wouldn't be related to old Bigfoot Wallace, would he?" asked Longarm.

The outlaw called Dutchy snorted. "Don't let Heck hear you askin' that question, Parker. Growin' up in Texas with the name of Wallace, he heard about Bigfoot ever since he was a sprout."

"He's sick of it," said Van Horn. "And no, he ain't related. Are you related to Quanah Parker?"

Longarm laughed and said, "There's no Comanche blood in me that I know of. I came out here from West-by-God Virginia after the Late Unpleasantness, and we didn't have too many Comanch' back there."

"Well, you look a little like an Indian," said Dutchy. He turned to Funderburk. "Don't he?"

Funderburk just grunted. He hadn't said more than three words since Longarm had ridden up to join the group. The outlaw called Graydon was a little more talkative, but not much.

Longarm was aching to know which of the outlaws had grabbed Nora Canady and why. He suspected it had been Heck Wallace himself; the leader of the gang was more likely to have pulled such an audacious stunt. But he couldn't ask any questions about the stagecoach robbery, because as far as these men knew, he wasn't even aware of what had happened. All he could really do was talk idly until they reached the hideout.

Luckily, in his line of work, Longarm picked up much of the same gossip that the fellows who rode on the other side of the law heard in their travels. He was able to talk about who had pulled what job, who had been caught and hanged, who had been gunned down by star packers. Every such exchange strengthened his companions' belief that he was who he said he was. At least, he hoped so.

Darkness had fallen and the stars had come out, providing enough illumination for the riders to see where they were going. Once the moon rose and cast its silvery glow down over the sand hills, it would be almost as bright out here as on an overcast day.

Along with darkness had come a strengthening of the wind. It had a chill to it that was rather shocking compared to the heat of the day just past. Longarm knew from experience, though, how cold it could get on the desert at night. These sand hills were no different. By morning the temperature would be downright frigid.

Van Horn and the others expected to be at the outlaw camp before it got too cold, however, and sure enough, after another half hour of winding through the sand hills, a light appeared up ahead. It was a campfire, Longarm realized, built down in one of the low valleys between dunes so that it could not have been seen for more than a few hundred yards.

"Good," said Van Horn. "The other boys got back first

83

and started a fire. Sure hope they put some coffee on to boil.''

"And got some beans cookin','' added Dutchy. "I'm hungry,''

"You're always hungry, Dutchy,'' Graydon said.

"Now, that ain't true a-tall. Sometimes I'm asleep.''

Longarm couldn't help but chuckle. He reminded himself that he was riding with a group of men who were ruthless killers and thieves. True, Van Horn was sort of friendly, and Dutchy was a comical cuss, but that didn't really mean anything. They were still outlaws, and Longarm knew they would kill him in the blink of an eye if they knew he was really a lawman.

His badge and identification papers, tucked away in the leather folder inside his shirt pocket, seemed at times to be glowing white-hot, so that they melted right into his skin. But that was just his imagination, he told himself. Still, he wished he'd thought to hide them before joining up with the bandits. He knew a Texas Ranger who carried his badge in a hidden pocket inside his belt, and another who concealed his badge in a secret compartment in a pocket watch. Longarm wondered if he ought to look into something like that for himself.

And there was always the possibility that one of the other members of the gang would recognize him from a past encounter. Longarm couldn't do anything about that. He would just have to take his chances.

Problem was, Nora Canady's chances were inextricably linked with his at the moment.

The five men rode down a long, gentle slope toward the camp. As they approached, Longarm saw by the light of the rising moon that a crude corral had been rigged by tying ropes to some of the dwarfish shin oaks. Four horses were in the corral, but five figures were visible around the fire. Three of them were moving around, each busy with some errand, while another hunkered on his heels next to the fire and fried something in a big pan over the flames.

The fifth and final figure sat on the sand on the opposite side of the fire, knees drawn up, head down, the very picture of dejection.

Nora, thought Longarm. It had to be.

"Better let me do the talking when we ride in, Parker," Van Horn warned him. "And keep your hands in plain sight and don't make any fast moves. The boys are liable to be spooked pretty easy right now, after nearly running head-on into that ambush this afternoon."

"You've got me to thank that you didn't," Longarm reminded him.

"And I'll be sure everybody knows that."

The three men who had been up and moving around all came to the edge of the camp to greet the newcomers. Obviously, they could all count and knew there was a stranger among the group riding in. They stood with their hands resting on their guns.

"Hello, the camp," Van Horn sang out to identify himself. "We're comin' in, boys."

"Who's that with you, Van Horn?" asked one of the outlaws.

"A friend . . . so he says." Van Horn reined his horse to a stop, and the men with him followed suit. "He claims he's the man who fired those warning shots when that posse was about to bushwhack us."

Longarm smelled the scent of bacon coming from the big frying pan. Even under the tense circumstances, the delicious aroma made him realize how long it had been since he'd eaten. Maybe he and Dutchy had something in common.

The man at the fire put the pan aside and straightened to his full height. He was a burly, barrel-chested man with a black Stetson shoved back on graying hair. When he spoke, his voice was like the rattle from a keg of rusty nails.

"And just because he said that, you brought the son of a bitch here? What the hell's the matter with you, Van Horn?"

Van Horn stiffened. "He says he wants to join up with us, Heck."

Heck Wallace moved his hand toward the gun on his hip. "And I say maybe I oughta plug the both of you, right here and now."

Longarm tensed, thinking that he might have to go for his own gun, when something happened that made all the men forget the confrontation for the moment.

The young woman sitting beside the fire began to sob, loudly and miserably.

Chapter 11

Wallace cursed and swung around toward the young woman. "Aw, now, don't start that yowlin' again," he said. "I've already promised you we ain't goin' to hurt you."

Slowly, Nora's sobs subsided. It was all Longarm could do to stay sitting easy in his saddle as he nodded toward her and asked casually, "Woman trouble?"

"Shut up," snapped Wallace as he turned back toward Longarm. "Let's see, I was just about to kill you, wasn't I?"

"If you want to shoot the fella who saved your hide and the hides of all your men from that ambush this afternoon, then go ahead," Longarm said coolly.

"So that was you, huh? Got any proof of that?"

"If I hadn't been there, how would I even know about it?"

"Maybe you're one o' them damned Rangers, tryin' to trick us," said Wallace. His hand was resting lightly on the butt of his Colt, which was cocked forward in its holster.

"Not hardly." Longarm inclined his head toward Van Horn and his companions. "Ask Van Horn and the boys. They'll tell you I joined up with them by cutting in from the west. That posse or whatever it was was a good ways back to the south. If I was a lawman, I couldn't have caught up to them as quickly as I did."

"That makes sense, Heck," ventured Van Horn. His neck might be on the line too, or at least his standing within the gang. He had to convince Wallace he had done the right thing by bringing Longarm here to the hideout in the sand hills.

Dutchy added, "He sure don't talk like no star packer, Heck. He says he's been ridin' with Lem Pollard up in Wyoming."

"Pollard got gunned down in Cheyenne a few weeks ago," Wallace said.

Longarm nodded. "That's right. And I nearly got killed right along with him. Me and a couple of other boys made it out of town one jump ahead of the law. I figured I'd better light out of Wyoming and find me some greener pastures."

For a long moment, Wallace didn't say anything. Then he blew out a deep breath through the bushy salt-and-pepper mustache that hung over his mouth. "All right," he said. "What's your name again, mister?"

"Parker," Longarm told him.

"All right, Parker, I won't kill you . . . yet. But you best be tellin' the truth. I don't cotton to bein' lied to, 'specially by no-good lawmen. You try anything funny, and you'll die long and hard."

Longarm swung down from the dun's saddle. "Much obliged for the hospitality," he said dryly. "Don't worry, Wallace. Only thing funny I know is Dutchy's appetite."

One of the other outlaws brayed with laughter. "Say, Parker here has got you figured out already, Dutchy," he gibed.

Longarm joined the others in leading their horses over to the makeshift corral. The other outlaws watched him fairly closely as he tended to the dun, then returned to the fire. Wallace had a pot of beans simmering over the flames now. It was unusual to see the leader of a gang doing the cooking, but evidently that was what Wallace preferred. He took some wild onions from a small bag, chopped them up with his

Bowie knife, and dropped them in the pot to cook with the beans. That made the blend of aromas floating in the air smell even better.

Longarm hunkered near the fire, enjoying the warmth of the crackling flames. That also gave him a chance to get a better look at Nora Canady. Even though her head was down, he could see enough of her face to know this was undoubtedly her. He recognized the pert nose, the full, slightly pouty lips. Even with tear-streaked cheeks and her hair hanging loosely around her face, she was damned close to beautiful. She wore a dark brown traveling dress, and high-buttoned shoes peeked out from under the hem.

She must have felt his eyes watching her, because she slowly lifted her head and stared straight at him. Aware that Wallace was still regarding him with suspicion, Longarm reached up and tugged on the brim of his hat as he gave Nora a brief nod. "Ma'am," he said, not overly polite but not cold either. He tried to give off the air of a man who was reserving judgment on everything until he knew what was going on.

"Can . . . can you help me?"

This was the first time Longarm had heard Nora's voice. It was low and hoarse from the crying she had been doing. He glanced toward Wallace, then said, "Well, ma'am, I don't rightly know. What is it that you need?"

Before Nora could answer, Wallace said, "What she needs is to hush up and quit complainin'. She ain't been harmed, and I've told her she won't be hurt if she just cooperates with us. Like tellin' me her name."

"You don't even know her name?" Longarm said, sounding surprised.

"How the hell could I?" demanded Wallace. "I only grabbed her this afternoon, and since then she ain't done any real talkin'." He looked at Nora and went on. "If you'd just tell me who you are and how to get hold of your pa or your husband, we could start talkin' about how they're goin' to buy you back from us."

So that was it, thought Longarm. Nora was wearing a fairly expensive outfit, and when the stagecoach was robbed she could have been carrying some fancy jewelry or something like that, something that had told Wallace she came from a wealthy background. Quite possibly, kidnapping her had been a spur-of-the-moment thing, with no deeper motivation than Wallace wanting to collect some ransom money.

Even though Longarm understood all of that, he pretended not to. Instead, he knelt there by the fire with a slightly baffled look on his face. It was perfectly all right with him if Wallace and the other outlaws thought he was a little bit slow on the uptake.

"Ma'am, if I was you, I'd do what Mr. Wallace says and cooperate with him," Longarm told Nora.

She just gave him a look of bitter disappointment, shook her head slightly, and went back to staring at the fire in front of her.

"Told you, Parker," said Wallace. "This gal's as stubborn as any female I've ever run across. And I've known some mule-headed ones, let me tell you."

"Ain't they all?" asked Dutchy, who had come up to the fire in time to hear Wallace's comment. "Women always smile so sweet and say"—his voice went up into a falsetto— " 'Whatever you want, sweetheart, it's up to you.' Then they blister your balls good an' proper if you don't do just exactly what they think you oughta." The other outlaws laughed.

Longarm smiled faintly, but kept any comments to himself. He tended to give the ladies a mite more credit than that, but he didn't want to get into an argument on his first— and hopefully last—night as a member of the Wallace gang.

Van Horn came up alongside Longarm and said, "Fetch your cup, Parker, and try some of the boss's coffee."

"Sounds good," said Longarm as he straightened. He added to Wallace, "Smells good too."

The outlaw leader just grunted and stirred the pot of beans. Longarm got a battered tin cup from his saddlebags, and Van Horn filled it from an equally battered pot. The coffee was so hot and strong Longarm suspected it would eat right through the tin if he gave it half a chance.

Wallace started dishing up the food. The members of the gang crowded around to be served. Longarm hung back a little, regarding the knot of men in front of him and wondering if he could get the drop on all of them at once if he pulled his gun.

That would be too risky, he decided. He would never be able to convince Nora of who he really was and get both of them mounted on horses and out of the camp without at least one of the gang trying to stop them. He didn't want any shooting at all if he could help it.

Wallace handed him a bowl of beans with several strips of bacon lying on top. Longarm took it and sat down cross-legged by the fire, like the other members of the gang had done. Everyone was eating except Wallace and Nora. Van Horn looked up from his bowl and asked, "I reckon Phil's comin' in later for his supper?"

"Yeah, you'll take his place after while," said Wallace.

That brief exchange told Longarm quite a bit. There was another member of the gang he hadn't seen yet, a man named Phil, and the only logical reason for his absence was that he was standing guard duty somewhere out there in the darkness. He was probably serving as an outrider, endlessly circling the camp on the lookout for anyone who might be searching for the outlaws. So even if Longarm had gotten Nora away from the camp earlier, as he had considered trying to do, he still would have had to deal with the man on guard. That was something to remember for the future as well.

Wallace dipped more beans in a bowl, added bacon to them, and carried the bowl over to Nora. She didn't look up at him, didn't even acknowledge that he was there.

"Here you go, ma'am," Wallace said to her. "You'd best eat."

Still without looking up, she said, "I don't want any." Her voice was a whisper.

"It's mighty good, ma'am," Dutchy told her. "And you need to keep your strength up."

"Why?" asked Nora, and her voice was a little louder now. "So I won't faint while you're . . . while you're all assaulting me?"

She was afraid she was going to be raped, Longarm realized, which was a pretty logical fear for a woman such as her under these circumstances. City-bred as she was, she probably knew little of the rough code of conduct that governed most frontiersmen, even owlhoots like these.

"Nobody's goin' to hurt you," said Wallace. "I've told you that before, ma'am, and I reckon I'll keep on sayin' it until you get it through your head. Hell, we ain't Comanches." Wallace knelt and thrust the bowl of beans at her. "Besides, it wouldn't make sense. Your pa or your husband will be a lot more likely to pay your ransom if he knows you ain't been touched."

Finally, Nora lifted her head a little so that she could look through hooded eyelashes at Wallace. After a moment, she reached out tentatively and took the bowl of food from him. She spooned up a few of the beans and put them in her mouth. After a moment, she nodded. "They're good."

Wallace's craggy face split in a grin. Clearly, he appreciated the compliment.

Longarm kept eating, and he had to agree with Nora's assessment: The food *was* good. He washed it down with more of the strong coffee, and when he was finished he slid a cheroot from his shirt pocket and lit it with a twig from the fire. Under other circumstances, he would have felt contented, maybe even a little lazy.

As it was, though, a part of his brain remained alert and razor-sharp, no matter what he might look like on the outside. When his chance came, he would have to be ready to seize it.

Nora ate with surprising gusto, considering that she had been snatched off a stagecoach a few hours earlier and brought to this camp of ruthless killers. That was the way of things, Longarm mused. The belly had its own schedule, and it didn't care overmuch what else was happening in the immediate vicinity.

When Nora had finished the food, she handed the empty bowl back to Wallace. "Thank you," she said.

"You're welcome."

"I . . . I might like a cup of that coffee. . . ."

Van Horn sprang to the pot. "Comin' up."

Dutchy said, "Ma'am, why don't you let me spread a saddle blanket on the ground so's you won't have to sit right on the sand like that?"

"That would be . . . very nice," said Nora. She got to her feet and brushed off her dress as Dutchy hurried to make good on his offer. Van Horn handed her a cup, and she sipped gratefully at the coffee.

"Sorry we don't have no cream or sugar for it," Van Horn told her.

"It's fine," she assured him. "A bit . . . potent . . . but very good."

Given half a chance, thought Longarm, this gang of hard-bitten desperadoes would be falling all over themselves to make Nora feel more comfortable around them. It was almost humorous watching them trying to impress her. That came from weeks, sometimes even months, of going without seeing any female face, let alone one as pretty as Nora's. Now that she had gotten the tearful silences out of the way, she was evidently starting to realize that she didn't have anything to fear from them, at least not immediately.

She settled back down on the blanket that Dutchy spread for her. As she sat there nursing the cup of coffee, Wallace sat down next to her and said, "Now, ma'am, surely you can see that we don't mean you any harm. So why don't you go ahead and tell us what we want to know."

"I . . . I don't understand," Nora said slowly. "You seem to think that I'm from a wealthy family."

"Well, what with the clothes you're wearin', and them rings you had on and that fancy watch you were carryin', it

93

seemed to me that you've got plenty of money. Or your man does anyway."

"I . . . I'm not married."

"Well, then, your pa's rich then. Bound to be."

She shook her head. "You're wrong. My father works for the railroad."

That was true enough in its way, thought Longarm, though some people would probably say that the railroad worked for Bryce Canady.

"He's a baggage clerk," said Nora.

"Then where'd you get the money for that jewelry?" demanded Wallace.

Nora pushed her hair back from her face. "I earned it. I earned it myself."

"Doin' what?" asked Dutchy.

Nora's lips curved in what she probably thought was a sensuous smile.

Oh, hell, Longarm thought as he leaned forward. *Don't say it. For God's sake, don't say it!*

"How does a working girl usually earn her money?" said Nora.

That did it, Longarm knew. That changed everything.

And now, somebody was probably going to die before this night was over.

Chapter 12

Wallace's eyes narrowed suspiciously under his bushy brows. "Are you sayin' you're a whore?" he asked bluntly.

Nora caught her breath, perhaps a little surprised at the vehemence of the outlaw leader's reaction. "I . . . I . . ." She looked around at the other men, clearly at a loss as to what to say or do next. She had to see the same thing that Longarm saw in the eyes of the men. They would fuss over her and pet her as long as they thought her safe return might get them a good payoff. If she was just another soiled dove, pretty and fancy-dressed though she might be, then she was good for only one thing as far as they were concerned.

"What about it, lady?" Van Horn asked quietly.

That was when Longarm said excitedly, "Damn it, I knew I'd seen her before!"

Dutchy asked, "Did she work in a whorehouse you went to, Parker? How was she?"

Longarm shook his head and said with conviction, "She's no soiled dove, boys. Her picture was all over the Denver papers when I came through there a few days ago."

Nora began to look even more aghast than she had a moment earlier.

"This little lady is Miss Nora Canady," Longarm said, pressing on. "In case you don't recognize the name, her daddy is Bryce Canady, that railroad tycoon who's got more money than God!''

''Nooo!'' Nora wailed as tears welled from her eyes again. ''He's lying!''

Longarm shook his head. ''No, I'm not,'' he insisted. ''Look at her. Look how's she acting. She knows I'm telling the truth. Her father's one of the richest men west of the Mississippi!''

Desperate times called for desperate measures, or so the old saying went, Longarm told himself. He just hoped these desperate measures didn't add up to one of the biggest mistakes he'd ever made in his life.

Wallace glowered at Nora and said, ''Is it true? Are you Canady's daughter?''

Nora shook her head, the gesture almost violent in its intensity. ''Of course not. This man is lying. I . . . I'm a whore, just like you said—''

''Look at her,'' Longarm cut in scornfully. ''I reckon we've all known our share of calico cats, boys. Does this gal look like one of them to you?''

''Parker's got a point,'' said Dutchy. ''I never seen a soiled dove quite so . . . refined-looking.''

''Hell,'' said Van Horn, ''I've known whores who thought they were ladies, but I never knew a lady who thought she was a whore. Why would a woman claim such a thing if it wasn't true?''

Longarm was wondering the same thing. Clearly, Nora had wanted to conceal her true identity, even if it meant letting these men think she was a prostitute. But just as clearly, she hadn't thought that strategy all the way through; otherwise she would have known the kind of reaction it would likely provoke in them. Her lie must have been an impulse, but at this point, Longarm still didn't know what had prompted it.

Nor was her motive in lying of much importance. What mattered was convincing the outlaws that Nora was still worth more to them unmolested.

"Seems like I read in the paper that she had disappeared from Denver," Longarm said. "I know I remember something about a reward being offered."

"A reward?" echoed Wallace. "What sort of reward are you talkin' about?"

"A big one," Longarm said simply.

Nora stared at him for a second, then dropped her face into her hands and began crying again. Her miserable sobs were the only thing that broke the tense silence around the campfire.

After a moment, Wallace said, "Well, it looks to me like Parker must be right. If this gal is really Bryce Canady's daughter, then we've stumbled onto a pure-dee gold mine, boys. We'll make him pay through the nose to get her back. But she's got to go back untouched, if you get my meanin'."

"I reckon we all do," said Van Horn. He sounded disappointed but accepting of Wallace's decree. Nora would not be harmed.

Longarm sat back. He had headed off this immediate problem, but that didn't mean he was out of the woods yet. He still had to figure out a way to get Nora away from the outlaws, because he didn't trust Wallace and the others to protect her, even though they hoped to collect a big ransom for her. Too many things could go wrong, and Nora could wind up dead if she was left in their hands.

"No point in all that cryin', ma'am," Wallace told her. "You're better off now than you were before Parker spilled the beans about you, whether you know it or not." Wallace glanced at Longarm. "You're sure about all this, Parker?"

Longarm nodded. "I'm sure. I wouldn't lie to you, Wallace."

"Well, now, I don't reckon I know you well enough to be convinced of that just yet, Parker. But I'll admit, it's startin' to look like maybe we can trust you."

Nora couldn't say the same thing. When she glanced up at Longarm, her eyes still wet with tears, she looked daggers at him. He met her gaze squarely, hoping that she would understand once he got a chance to explain why he'd done what he did.

After a few minutes, several of the men started yawning. Graydon announced that he was going to turn in. Wallace said, "Somebody kick in a couple of spare blankets. We'll make a bedroll for Miss Canady."

Dutchy and Van Horn provided the blankets, which didn't surprise Longarm. They seemed to be the most taken with Nora. She accepted the bedding with no thank-you this time; apparently, her idea of playing up to her captors had been abandoned.

As Longarm spread his own bedroll, the man called Phil rode in to the camp for supper. Van Horn saddled his horse and rode out to take Phil's place.

"Who's that?" Phil asked as he scooped the last of the beans out of the pot. He was looking at Longarm.

"Fella's name is Parker," Wallace said. "Wants to join up with us. He claims he's the one who helped us out when that posse was about to jump us this afternoon. And since he rode down through Denver recent-like, he was able to tell us who that gal is."

Phil was a tall, slender man with curly dark hair under a pushed-back Stetson. "Is that so?"

"Yep. She's the daughter of that railroad baron, Bryce Canady."

Phil let out a low whistle. "Sounds like you're earnin' your keep already, Parker. Pleased to meet you."

"Likewise," Longarm said with a curt nod. "Now, if you fellas don't mind, I'm going to get some sleep."

He stretched out, rolled in his blankets, and closed his eyes. But he didn't fall asleep. In fact, he had never felt less like sleeping in his entire life, he thought. He listened intently to the low-voiced conversation between Wallace and Phil.

"Any sign of those Rangers, or sheriff's deputies, or whatever they were?" asked Wallace.

"Nope. The night's mighty quiet, Heck. Anyway, those

lawmen couldn't find this camp if they wandered around the sand hills for a year.''

''Unless they got lucky.'' Wallace grunted. ''Could happen.''

''Not likely. I don't reckon there's a white man alive who knows these dunes like you do.'' Phil paused, then asked, ''What're we goin' to do with the girl?''

''I figure we've got to get hold of her pa some way and let him know we've got her. Van Horn can write a little. Maybe he can write a letter to the old man, and one of us can take it into Monahans to mail it.''

''If Parker's just come down from the north, likely nobody in Monahans would recognize him,'' suggested Phil.

''That's a thought,'' agreed Wallace. ''Well, we'll see. All I know right now is that little gal's goin' to make us all rich men.''

Not if he had anything to say about it, thought Longarm.

It wasn't long before everyone had turned in for the night. The fire burned down to embers, and without its glow, the landscape once again took on a silvery hue from the moonlight and starlight. Longarm opened his eyes to mere slits and concentrated on watching Nora. She was restless, tossing and turning in the borrowed soogans. The outlaws all seemed to be sleeping soundly. Loud snores issued from several of them. Longarm waited, though, biding his time in case any of them were shamming, like he was. The moon gradually slid down through the heavens and dropped behind the dunes, making the darkness grow much deeper. Soundlessly, Longarm slid his blankets aside.

He had taken his boots off before he turned in, so he didn't have to worry about his spurs clanking as he crawled noiselessly across the sand toward Nora. She had turned over in her sleep so that her face was toward him, and he was grateful for that. He intended to clamp a hand over her mouth as soon as he reached her so that she couldn't make any startled outcry when he woke her.

Longarm paused every few feet to make sure none of the men were stirring. Finally, after what seemed like an hour, he reached Nora's blanket-wrapped shape. He slid close to her, then dropped his weight on her, pinning her down so that she couldn't thrash around. At the same time, he covered her mouth with his big left hand.

He saw starlight glitter on her eyes as they opened wide in shock. Moving his head so that his lips were against her ear, he breathed, "Don't move, and don't yell. I'm not an outlaw. I'm U.S. Deputy Marshal Custis Long." He doubted if the words could be heard more than a foot away.

He didn't know if what he was saying penetrated Nora's brain. Her body had heaved once in fright, but she hadn't been able to move much because of his weight pressing down on her. After that, she lay still, panting slightly. He could feel each exhalation of breath against his palm.

After a few long seconds ticked by, she gave a tiny nod, barely jerking her head up and down. Longarm took that to mean she understood what he had told her. He whispered, "Don't yell now. Don't even talk. Just listen to me. I'm here to get you out of this mess and take you home."

Another nod.

"We can't get away tonight. We'll have to wait another day or two, until they trust me more. Can you do that?"

A nod, immediate and emphatic.

"All right. Just be brave. They won't hurt you, and if they try to, I'll stop them. Just do what I tell you and be ready to move fast when the time comes, and before you know it you'll be back with your father and Senator Palmer."

He felt something wet trickle onto the back of his hand. She was crying again, and one of her tears had fallen on him. Tears of gratitude this time, Longarm thought.

He took his hand away from her mouth and squeezed her shoulder briefly through the blankets to reassure her, then slid off her and began crawling back to the spot where he had been pretending to sleep. He glanced around at the other forms stretched out on the sand. None of them were moving,

100

and the snores had continued unabated while he was whispering to Nora. He reached his bedroll and slipped back into it, confident that none of the outlaws were aware of his nocturnal ramblings. The marks that his hands and knees had left in the sand would be gone by morning, swept away by the ceaseless wind.

Longarm let himself doze a little then, sleeping lightly so that he could be instantly awake if need be. It was a skill he had developed over years of being a manhunter and finding himself in places where he couldn't afford to sleep deeply, yet still needed some rest.

He knew when Van Horn rode in, far into the night, and roused Funderburk to go take his place as outrider. Van Horn curled up in his blankets, broke wind a couple of times, and fell asleep immediately. Nothing else disturbed the camp until the faint grayness that warned of dawn's approach began to seep into the eastern sky. Longarm let himself drift off completely then, and he slept soundly for an hour, waking to the smell of coffee being brewed.

Wallace was the only one who was up and about. He had rekindled the fire and had the flames leaping merrily again. The coffeepot was bubbling at the edge of the fire. The other outlaws were starting to stir. Longarm sat up, stretched, and reached for his boots.

As he did so, he glanced at Nora. She was lying down, but her eyes were wide open. She was staring at him. He wished she wouldn't do that. It looked suspicious, and if she kept it up, Wallace or one of the others might start to wonder why she was paying so much attention to him.

Longarm shook his boots out to make sure no scorpions had crawled into them during the night, pulled them on, stood up, and stamped his feet down in them good. The other men were all awake by now. Dutchy was sitting up and scratching himself. "Mornin', boys," he mumbled.

Wallace had broken out the frying pan and bags of flour, sugar, and salt, along with a canteen of water. He began mixing batter for flapjacks.

Longarm wandered off behind one of the small dunes. He hoped that would serve a dual purpose. He needed to take a leak, and he hoped that leaving for a moment would get Nora's attention off him. They couldn't afford for her to be showing more interest in him than in any of the others.

When he had 'finished relieving himself, he buttoned his trousers and strolled back around the dune to the campsite. All the men were up now, some of them tending to the horses, others helping themselves to coffee. Longarm got his cup and joined them, taking the pot from Van Horn to pour himself some of the steaming brew. No one else was ready for coffee, so Longarm knelt to place the pot near the edge of the fire, so that the flames would keep it hot.

Nora sat up and said, "He's a lawman."

Wallace's head jerked up, and the frying pan clattered against the rocks that had been ringed around the fire. "What?"

Longarm couldn't believe his ears. He must have imagined hearing what Nora had just said.

But then she said it again. "He's a lawman, a U.S. deputy marshal. He crawled over to my bedroll and told me so last night after all the rest of you were asleep."

Longarm was still hunkered down by the fire. Wallace was only a few feet away staring at him with a mixture of disbelief, suspicion, and anger. Van Horn, Dutchy, and one of the other men stood nearby. Graydon and the others were over at the corral, and Funderburk hadn't come in from his stint of standing guard.

"Well?" Wallace said harshly. "What about it, Parker?"

"His name isn't Parker," Nora said before Longarm could say anything. "It's Long, Custis Long. That's what he told me."

Why the hell was she doing this? Why betray him, thought Longarm, when he was her best chance of getting out of this mess alive and unharmed?

"Long," Wallace said, and then his eyes widened in shock

as a realization hit him. "Son of a bitch, you're the one they call Longarm!"

For an instant, Longarm thought about trying to talk his way out of this, but then he realized he wasn't going to be able to do that. Wallace was already reaching for his gun. So Longarm did the only thing he could do.

He threw the potful of scalding coffee right in Wallace's face.

Chapter 13

Wallace howled in pain and clawed at his burned face with both hands as he fell over backward. In a continuation of the same motion he had used to throw the coffee at Wallace, Longarm swung the now-empty pot as he uncoiled from his crouch. Dutchy was within reach, and the pot clanged loudly as Longarm crashed it against the side of the stocky outlaw's head. Dutchy went down like a poleaxed steer.

The other men were shouting curses and grabbing for their guns. None of them were particularly fast on the draw, however, and Longarm cleared leather first, palming the Colt from the cross-draw rig and thumbing back the hammer as the barrel came level with his waist. He fired from there, flame licking from the muzzle of the revolver. The bullet drove into the chest of the man standing next to Van Horn. Longarm had never caught his name the night before, but that didn't matter. He had just killed the outlaw anyway.

Van Horn snapped a shot at Longarm that whistled past the big lawman's ear. Longarm fired again, but as he squeezed the trigger, Van Horn ducked aside. Longarm's slug still creased Van Horn's arm, knocking the owlhoot around in a half-turn. Longarm used the opportunity to step closer and swing a rock-hard left fist at Van Horn, planting the punch in the middle of the man's face. Van Horn dropped his gun and fell back, stunned.

Longarm had been mighty lucky so far, and he knew it. He threw a glance at Nora, who was sitting up and screaming, hands clapped over her ears to shut out some of the sounds of gunfire. Longarm started to take a step toward her, thinking about snatching her up from the ground, but Graydon was running toward Nora from the corral, gun drawn. Longarm knew he couldn't reach her before the outlaw did.

The horses were milling around in the makeshift corral, spooked by the shooting and the yelling. Two of the outlaws were still there, trying to calm the nervous animals. Longarm fired over the heads of the horses and bellowed at them at the top of his lungs, and sure enough, they bolted, surging against the ropes and bursting right through them. The two outlaws were caught in the miniature stampede and knocked sprawling.

Longarm lunged toward the horses as Graydon reached Nora and fired past her at the lawman, making her flinch and scream even louder. The slug burned across Longarm's right side, just above his belt. He stumbled, thrown off balance by the impact of the bullet, even though it had only dug a shallow furrow in his flesh. Pain flashed through him, but he thrust it away, ignoring it as he leaped for the dun.

He caught hold of the horse's mane with both hands and kicked off with his feet, trying to throw a leg over the back of the animal. The Pony Express riders had been able to mount up that way, but they had all been young and small and wiry. Longarm was big and rangy and no longer in the first flush of youth.

But he *was* desperate, and that desperation gave him speed and strength he might not have otherwise had. He slammed down on the dun's bony back and felt a twinge in his recently recovered balls. Then he was leaning forward, knees clamped to the horse's flanks, one hand tangled in the dun's mane, the other wielding the Colt. He yelled encouragement to the dun as he sent it straight toward the fire.

The dun jumped, sailing up and over the flames without hesitation. Longarm lashed out at Graydon as the horse came down next to the outlaw and Nora. The barrel of Longarm's pistol thudded against Graydon's skull. Longarm hated treating a perfectly good gun that way and hoped the blow hadn't bent the barrel. But Graydon folded up like a house of cards, and that was more important to Longarm at the moment. He bent down and looped an arm around Nora as she leaped to her feet. He had to use his gun hand to do it, but he was able to pick her up and pull her onto the horse with him as it surged past the fallen outlaw.

"Hang on!" Longarm shouted to Nora. "We'll get out of here!"

She twisted in his arms, clawed at his face with her fingernails, and generally started fighting like a blamed wildcat.

That surprised Longarm, but not completely. After all, she had already betrayed him to the outlaws this morning, for reasons that he still couldn't fathom. Obviously, she didn't want to go with him, didn't want to be rescued despite her fear of Wallace and the other men.

He struggled with her, trying to calm her, as the dun lurched up one of the sand dunes that surrounded the camp. A gun boomed somewhere behind them, and then Longarm heard Wallace bellowing, "Don't shoot! Don't shoot, you stupid bastards! You'll hit the girl!"

She was his ace in the hole, all right, thought Longarm.

Just then, she dug her elbow hard into the wound on his side.

Longarm gasped in agony and bent forward as the whole world seemed to turn black and red for a second. Mostly black, with bright streaks of red running through it. That was the color of pain, he thought.

Nora writhed in his grasp, then hit him again in the side, followed by ramming the heel of her hand under his chin. Her fighting was clumsy but effective. Longarm almost toppled off the horse. He caught himself at the last instant.

But he couldn't catch Nora. She tore free from him and

fell off the back of the dun just as the horse crested the dune. She landed hard and started rolling over and over, tumbling down the steep slope of the sand hill. Still half-blinded by pain, Longarm yanked the dun to a momentary halt and hipped around to look back at Nora. The skirt of her traveling gown had hiked up over her hips as she rolled down the hill, and Longarm saw the flash of pale skin from her legs in the half-light of dawn. Van Horn and one of the other men were already running toward the base of the dune to grab her when her rolling finally came to a stop.

"Kill him! Kill the son of a bitch!"

That was Wallace giving the orders. Guns began to bang again. Now that he no longer had Nora with him, the outlaws had no reason not to shoot at Longarm. They opened up with a vengeance, their guns blazing as they sent lead whistling up the slope toward Longarm. He heard the all too familiar flat slap of a bullet passing close beside his ear as he turned and dug his heels into the dun's flanks. The horse leaped forward into an awkward gallop as it went down the far side of the sand hill.

The other horses had scattered, and that fact gave Longarm his only advantage. He was the only one mounted. It would take the outlaws quite a while to round up their frightened mounts—he hoped. Longarm rode west, trying to keep the dun to the more solid ground so that he could make better time. With the lead he had, he at least had a chance to get away from the Wallace gang.

But he'd had to leave Nora behind, and that fact gnawed at his guts. Sure, turning around and trying to go back to rescue her right now would be suicide, just as sure as if he'd put the barrel of his own gun in his mouth and pulled the trigger. Wallace and the others would kill him on sight.

At least Nora was safe for the moment, as safe as she had been since Wallace had grabbed her off that stagecoach. He would just have to find some other way to get her away from those outlaws, Longarm told himself.

That was when a wave of dizziness and weakness hit him,

and he almost toppled off the back of the dun.

Longarm caught himself, pulled himself upright again, and gingerly touched a hand to the wound on his side. His shirt was soaked with blood, more blood than Longarm had thought he was losing. That was the reason he had almost blacked out. Gritting his teeth, he reached through the gap in the bullet-torn shirt and explored the wound. It was a little deeper than he had thought. Blood was still oozing from it, but slowly now, barely a trickle. The injury wasn't life-threatening, not by itself. But under the circumstances . . .

The sun had topped the horizon behind him. Its heat on his back told him that he was going in the direction he wanted to go. If he could get out of the sand hills, find the stage road, and follow it to Monahans, he could get help, both for his injury and for his next attempt to rescue Nora Canady.

Without him prodding it, the dun had settled down into a trudging walk through the sand. Longarm dug in his heels, urging the horse back to a faster pace. Wallace and the others might have caught their horses by now and could be coming after him. He was leaving a clear trail for them to follow. In the sand, there was no avoiding that.

On the other hand, they might not chase him. They might just take Nora and break camp, moving to somewhere deeper in the sand hills. That would probably be the smart thing for them to do. Wallace had successfully eluded pursuit for months now by hiding in the dunes. He could find another place to camp. Vengeance on Longarm would have to be weighed against the payoff the gang could get by selling Nora back to her tycoon father.

Longarm hoped greed would win out this time. He was in no shape to fight off a bunch of bloodthirsty owlhoots. He needed time . . . time to heal, time to make plans. . . .

The sun got hotter as it rose steadily into the sky behind him. Soon, it was like a hammer beating down on him. At least he had been wearing his hat when he escaped from the outlaw camp. The Stetson gave his head a little protection from the burning rays.

His mouth felt as if it was lined with wool, though. Even under normal circumstances, he would have been thirsty. With all the blood he had lost, he was in serious danger of passing out from lack of fluid.

And of course he had no canteen. That was back at the outlaw camp, along with his saddle, his rifle, and all the rest of his supplies. He had the dun, the clothes he was wearing, his Colt, and the dozen cartridges in the loops of his shell belt.

That would have to be enough.

The dun needed water too. Longarm knew that, but there was nothing he could do about it. All he could do was ride through the dunes . . . up one, down another, zigzagging back and forth to try to avoid the steepest slopes, always heading generally to the west.

Only when he looked up and saw that the sun was directly above him did he realize how long he had been riding. It was the middle of the day. He had gone far beyond mere thirst now. His whole body was screaming for water. He would have to take a chance and stop the next time he came to some of those shin oaks. Maybe he could scoop out a hole around the roots of the trees and find a little moisture that way.

A few minutes later, he spotted some of the diminutive trees and angled the dun toward them. They clustered in a narrow, low place between two dunes, and a little grass even grew around the trunks of the trees. Longarm brought the horse to a stop and slid off its back, holding tight to the mane to keep himself from falling all the way to the ground. He took several deep breaths, the hot, arid air burning his lungs. When he felt strong enough and steady enough, he stepped away from the dun and lowered himself to his knees beside one of the oaks. Using both hands, he began to dig around its base, scooping out the sand and flinging it behind him. Digging should have been easy, he thought, but somehow it wasn't. It seemed like more sand fell into the hole from the sides than he was taking out of it.

But gradually, the hole deepened, and when Longarm plunged his hands into the sand at the bottom of it, he thought the grains felt slightly damp. They seemed to cling together more.

That was enough to give him a burst of renewed energy. He dug faster, trying not to let himself become frantic. Pawing at the dirt like a madman would just waste energy, and he couldn't afford to do that.

Suddenly the dun was beside him, sticking its nose in the hole and butting at him. Longarm swatted the horse's muzzle and shooed it away. That confirmed what he had thought. The dun smelled water; otherwise it wouldn't have acted like that.

"Hang on, old son," he rasped, his voice sounding strange to his ears as it came from his dry throat. "Maybe in a few minutes there'll be water enough for both of us."

Longarm leaned forward and reached down into the hole. The sand was mud now. He pushed it aside, making a little hollow, and watched in fascination as a little water seeped into the depression, forming a tiny pool a few inches wide. A sound that was almost a sob came from deep inside Longarm. With fumbling fingers, he pulled his bandanna from the pocket of his trousers and lowered it into the hole, letting it soak up the water. Then he lifted it, tipped his head back, and squeezed the precious drops from the cloth into his open mouth.

Dirty water had never tasted so good.

Longarm repeated the process several times, pausing to dig down a little deeper when the water stopped seeping into the hole. Then, when he felt stronger, he took the wet bandanna and stood up, using it to swab around the dun's dust-caked nose and mouth. He soaked up more of the water and squeezed it into his hat, then held that so the horse could drink.

"I reckon maybe we'll both make it out of here yet, old son," he said to the horse.

The sound of a shot split the air.

Longarm almost dropped his hat. The horse had finished sucking up the water in it anyway. Longarm clapped the Stetson back on his head and looked around, trying to figure out where the shot had come from. It had sounded close, but not right on top of him. Had the outlaws split up, and was the shot a signal from one of them to the others that he had found Longarm?

Longarm grabbed the dun's mane again and swung up onto its back. "Come on, hoss," he said hoarsely. "I'm sorry as hell about it, but we got to run again."

He urged the horse into a run, still heading west. At least, he hoped it was west. With the sun overhead now, it was harder to tell which direction he was going. He wished he could think more clearly. He didn't want to ride right back into his pursuers.

There hadn't been any more shots, only the one. Longarm had no idea what that fact meant. The horse plunged up the side of a dune, half-ran, half-slid down the far side. Longarm leaned forward, clutching the horse's mane, urging it on. Only gradually did he become aware that the dun was moving at a smoother gait, not lurching back and forth as it had to do in the grip of the sand. Longarm looked down at the ground in amazement, saw that the dun was running now over land that was still sandy, but not like before. This ground was harder and had more vegetation growing in it. Longarm twisted his head to look behind him. The dunes rose there, a few hundred yards back.

He was out of the sand hills!

He looked ahead of him again, and movement caught his eye. He saw a horse, a figure in a broad-brimmed hat standing beside the animal. He saw something in the figure's hands . . . a rifle.

And it started to come up and point toward him.

Not now! thought Longarm as he reached for his Colt. He couldn't have escaped from Wallace and the others only to run smack-dab into the mysterious man who had tried to kill him up in New Mexico Territory. . . .

Longarm had barely touched the butt of his gun when something crashed into his head and flung him into a darkness so deep that even the bright West Texas sun was no match for it.

Chapter 14

So this was what heaven was like, thought Longarm. A soft bed to lie in, a cool cloth bathing his brow, gentle hands lifting his head so that cold water could be trickled into his mouth and down his throat. He had halfway expected to wake up in the other place, but since it wasn't hot and he didn't hear the fiendish, cackling laughter of demons and imps, he supposed Saint Peter had taken pity on him and let him in through the Pearly Gates after all.

Then he choked on the water and came up off the bed, gagging and coughing. Red waves of pain coursed through him.

Now it started. He was in Hades after all, and the eternal torment was about to commence.

"It's all right," a voice said as Longarm's coughing fit diminished. "Take it easy, mister. Just lie back there and catch your breath."

That was a woman's voice, thought Longarm.

Satan was a *woman*?

He dragged his eyes open, and saw a face looming over him. It was a woman's face, all right, with wings of dark hair framing it. At the moment, lines of concern were etched on her forehead, but Longarm could tell that under better circumstances, she would be mighty attractive.

"You're too . . . pretty to be . . . the Devil," he croaked.

She blinked in surprise; then a faint smile curved her lips. "Thank you . . . I think," she said.

"Wh . . . where am . . ." Longarm was too weak to finish the sentence.

"You're in my bed," she told him bluntly. "Just lie still and rest. You've been through a lot."

"The fella who . . . shot me . . . where is he?"

"I don't know anything about that. All I know is that you came thundering out of the sand hills at me on that fire-eyed dun, and I was afraid you were going to ride me down. Then you acted like you were going to shoot me. You might have if you hadn't fallen off your horse."

Longarm looked past her and saw a hat hanging on a nail driven into the wall. It was a broad-brimmed hat, sort of like the one that had been worn by the bushwhacker with the Spencer carbine in Ashcroft, but not identical. Close enough, though, that Longarm had taken it for the same hat.

"I saw you . . . lift your rifle. . . ."

"Well, what would you do if some crazy man was riding straight at you like a bat out of hell?" The woman was starting to sound a little impatient now. "But I never shot you, mister. You fell off your horse, plain and simple, and knocked yourself out when you hit the ground."

Longarm let his head sag back against the pillow under it. His eyelids were so heavy that he couldn't hold them up any longer. But even as they slid shut, he asked, "Did you . . . see anybody else . . . out there?"

"You mean somebody chasing you? The same somebody who put that bullet crease in your side?"

"Yeah."

"Didn't see hide nor hair of them. Now, are you going to shut up and get some sleep? If you do, I'll have some food ready when you wake up."

Longarm's stomach lurched. Food was the last thing in the world he wanted right now. Sleep, though, that sounded

114

pretty good. He opened his mouth to tell the woman he would try to sleep.

He was out like a blown-out lamp before he could even form the words.

Longarm had no idea how long he had been asleep when he woke up again. He blinked several times and looked around the room. There was a small table beside the bed, and on it burned a lamp with the wick turned down low. The tiny flame gave off enough light for him to see that the walls of the room were adobe. The bed was big, a four-poster that took up nearly all the space in the room. It looked like it would have been more appropriate in a Southern plantation house, rather than some adobe hacienda in West Texas.

The room's single window had a curtain drawn across it. Longarm suspected it was night, because no light leaked in around the edges of the curtain.

Now that he had acquainted himself with his surroundings, he took stock of himself. He realized with a shock that he was naked except for some bandages wrapped tightly around his middle. The wound ached, but it didn't hurt too badly, even when he shifted around in the bed and sat up. Obviously, the woman had cleaned it and bound it up. She seemed to have done a good job of it too, which indicated that she'd had some experience in patching up bullet wounds.

An earthen pitcher sat on the table next to the lamp. Longarm reached over and picked it up, dipped his finger into the liquid in it, and tasted it. Water, sure enough. He lifted the pitcher to his mouth and took a long drink. That helped his thirst some, but he still felt as if he would never again be able to get enough to drink. He forced himself to set the pitcher back on the table anyway. Guzzling down a lot of water right now might make him sick.

He became aware that, contrary to his feelings earlier, he was hungry now. Ravenous, in fact. And the woman had promised to feed him if he got some rest. Well, he was rested now, and he wanted that food. He was about to call out for her when the door near the foot of the bed opened and she stepped into the room.

"Oh," she said as she paused just inside the door, holding a tray with a bowl on it. "You're awake. I was going to wake you if you weren't."

This was Longarm's first really good look at her, and he liked what he saw, enough so that her beauty even distracted him from the savory aromas drifting up from whatever was in that bowl.

At first glance, most men would have taken her for being in her early twenties, but Longarm added a few years onto that. She was less than thirty, though, he judged. Lean but not skinny, with ample curves in the right places. She wore a plain gray dress that was clean but old, with several patches on it. Her face had the deep tan that spoke of a life spent mostly outdoors, and as she came closer, Longarm saw that her hands were strong-looking, with nails cut short and blunt. Working hands, he thought.

Yet she did not have the haggard, worn-out look of a woman who had spent her entire life on the frontier. She had grown up somewhere else, he decided, but had been out here long enough for the hardscrabble life to begin taking a toll on her.

And her eyes were the blue of a deep mountain lake.

"I'm afraid all I have is stew," she said, dragging Longarm's attention back from her eyes.

"Stew sounds mighty fine," he told her.

"So, you have your appetite back now?"

"Yes, ma'am."

She smiled. "That's a good sign. I thought I was dragging you back from death's door, but maybe you weren't really quite that bad off."

"Bad enough," said Longarm. "I'm much obliged to you for helping me."

Carefully, she placed the tray across his lap. "Can you feed yourself?" she asked. "Or should I help you?"

"I'll give it a try," Longarm said as he reached for the spoon lying next to the bowl.

"Be careful. It's hot. If you spill it, you're liable to burn your . . . yourself."

He wondered if that was what she had really been about to say. And he reminded himself that he was naked under the sheet spread over him. If she was alone here, as she gave every sign of being, that meant she was the one who had taken his clothes off, cleaned him up, and gotten him into bed. Her bed, he recalled.

"My name is Beth Jellicoe," she blurted out.

"Long," he told her. "Custis Long. I'm mighty pleased to meet you, Miss Jellicoe."

"It's Mrs.," she said.

"Oh."

"I'm a widow."

That was information Longarm hadn't asked for, but she had been quick to volunteer it. He wasn't quite sure what to say in response, so he played it safe. "I'm sorry about your loss."

"It's been a while. Three years, in fact. Thomas was a good man. A horse kicked him, caved in his ribs. I couldn't save him."

"Sorry," Longarm said again.

She gestured at the bowl. "You'd better eat your stew while it's hot."

Longarm dug in, savoring the delicious blend of flavors. The chunks of chicken that floated in the stew were a little tough and stringy, but the vegetables were tender enough. As he ate, he could almost feel strength flowing back into him.

Beth Jellicoe sat down in a ladder-back chair with a cane bottom to watch him eat. She seemed to be enjoying it. She smiled in satisfaction when Longarm scraped up the last of the stew and spooned it into his mouth.

"I'm sorry I didn't have any bread for sopping. I have some biscuits cooking now. We can have them next time."

"It was mighty good, bread or no bread," Longarm told her honestly.

"What about coffee? Could you use a cup of coffee?"

He nodded. "That sounds plumb wonderful, ma'am."

She stood up and said, "I'll be right back."

He watched the sway of her hips with admiration as she left the room. Once she was gone, Longarm piled up the pillows behind him and leaned back to wait for her.

He wondered what this place was. A ranch, more than likely, he decided. And it was also likely that Beth's late husband had owned the ranch. After his death, she had stayed on for some reason. He wondered if they had had any children. He knew he hadn't heard any kids since he'd woken up, and it was difficult to keep youngsters that quiet for very long at a time.

Beth came back into the room carrying a cup of coffee. She handed it to Longarm and said, "I didn't know if you take cream and sugar or not, so I brought it black."

"Black's just fine, Miz Jellicoe." A dollop of Maryland rye would have made it even better, but Longarm kept that comment to himself for the time being. He didn't know if Beth had any liquor in the house and didn't want to be too forward about asking, not after all she done for him already.

The coffee was good, but it had a definite unexpected twist to its flavor. Longarm looked up after sipping it and said, "Chicory?"

Beth nodded. "I always put some in the pot when I brew coffee. An old habit."

"You're from New Orleans?"

Her face lit up with a smile. "That's right. You must know the city if you recognize the taste of chicory."

"Been there a time or two," Longarm admitted. He didn't add that the last time, he had gotten himself involved with a voodoo queen and had almost been killed by a damned zombie.

"I lived there until I was eighteen," she said. "Then I married Thomas and he decided to come out here and start

118

a ranch. We had a few good years until—" She stopped short and looked down at the floor. She had been talking easily to Longarm, and he regretted that she had suddenly felt uncomfortable. He waited quietly until she took a deep breath and went on. "You'll have to excuse me. I know I'm talking too much. It's just that I don't see very many people out here, and I don't get into town very often. It gets . . . lonely."

If there was one word to describe the Texas plains, that was it, thought Longarm. He nodded and said, "I know just what you mean, ma'am." He paused for a second, then asked, "Was that you who fired a shot not long before I came riding out of the sand hills like a crazy man?"

"That's right. I was shooting a jackrabbit." She nodded toward the empty bowl sitting on the bedside table. "I was glad I did, so we had some fresh meat."

Longarm swallowed hard. So that had been jackrabbit in the stew, not chicken. Well, it could have been worse, he told himself. Could have been rattlesnake.

"You run this ranch by yourself?"

"That's right," said Beth. "I might not admit that to a strange man under normal circumstances, but I happen to know that you're a lawman, so I suppose I can trust you."

"You found my badge and bona fides in my clothes?"

"Yes. And I have to admit that I'm very curious about why a United States deputy marshal would come galloping out of the sand hills with a bullet wound." She shook her head. "But I won't ask. I don't want to pry into things that are none of my business."

Longarm sipped more of the strong black coffee, then said, "I reckon you made it your business when you toted me in here and patched up that gully in my side, ma'am. You ever heard of the Heck Wallace gang?"

"Of course. Everyone in West Texas has heard of them lately, I imagine. Were they after you?"

Longarm nodded. "Yep. They've got something I want, and they didn't cotton to me trying to take it."

"Do you think they'll come here . . . looking for you?"

Longarm had asked himself that very question. He didn't want to put Beth in any danger. But it was entirely possible, even likely, that Wallace and the other outlaws had simply moved their camp and would not be coming after him. At the moment, they would be more interested in the ransom they hoped to get for Nora Canady than anything else.

"I don't think it's very likely," he said slowly in answer to Beth's question. "Did you see anybody else riding out of the sand hills?"

She shook her head. "No. And it took me a while to catch that dun of yours, then get you in the saddle on my horse. If the Wallace gang was chasing you, they weren't very close behind you."

That was good news, thought Longarm. It meant Beth was probably safe.

Of course, Nora was still in the hands of the gang, and he would have to deal with that, but at least he wouldn't have to worry about the outlaws showing up here at Beth's ranch and threatening her.

He said as much to Beth, leaving out any mention of Nora for the time being, and added, "If they do ride up, you'll have to turn me over to them."

She looked offended. "I'd never do that."

"You might not have any choice."

"I didn't haul you in here and patch up that bullet wound and feed you rabbit stew just so some outlaws can kill you, Custis Long," she said with a stubborn shake of her head. She stood up and came to take the bowl from the table. "Now, you'd better get some more rest."

He drained the last of the coffee from the cup and handed it to her as well. "Don't see as how that's very likely, not after that coffee," he said.

"Well, try anyway," she said tartly.

"Oh, all right." Might as well humor her, he thought. He

slid down in the bed and let his head sink in the pillows.

Damned if he didn't go to sleep, coffee or no coffee. He heard the door close softly behind her, and that was the last thing he was aware of for a long time.

Chapter 15

It was the next morning when Longarm awoke, and his bladder was hollering at him to give it some relief. He looked around for a chamber pot, and not seeing one, swung his legs out of bed and stood up to go in search of one.

That was when, despite having awakened feeling rested and refreshed, he was forcibly reminded that he had been wounded and lost a lot of blood only the day before. The room spun crazily around him. Hell, it felt like the whole world was spinning wrong. He let out a curse and grabbed one of the posts at the foot of the bed to keep from falling down.

A moment later, as his head was trying to settle down a little, the bedroom door opened and Beth Jellicoe stepped through it. "Good Lord!" she exclaimed when she saw him standing there clinging to the bedpost. "What are you doing up?"

"Needed to . . . answer the call of nature."

"Oh." Her eyes flicked downward to his groin. "I see." A smile tugged at her lips. "So that's the reason."

Longarm glanced down too, and saw that his shaft was sticking out long and hard in front of him. He felt an unexpected wave of embarrassment as he realized he was standing there stark naked except for the bandages around his middle, while Beth was fully dressed. It was a hell of a lot more comfortable being naked when the person with you was naked too.

Just the thought of Beth being naked caused his manhood to give a little jump, which made the embarrassment even worse. This wasn't the time for such shenanigans, he told himself sternly. He was still weak from that gunshot wound, blast it, and anyway he had a more urgent use for his member at the moment.

"Chamber pot?" he reminded Beth, who was still standing there smiling.

"Oh. Of course." She hurried around to the other side of the bed, reached underneath it, and brought back a porcelain pot. "Why don't you sit down on the edge of the bed, and I'll hold this—"

Longarm snatched the pot out of her hands. "Damn it, woman," he growled, "some things a fella wants to do for himself!"

"All right." He had a feeling she was trying hard not to laugh. "I'll be back in a few minutes with your breakfast. Flapjacks and bacon . . . and plenty of coffee."

He bit back a groan and shooed her out of the room.

He felt much better when she returned some five minutes later carrying a tray of food. He was back in the bed, the sheet pulled over him, and as she set the tray on the table, he asked, "Where's my clothes?"

"I have them, don't worry. Except for that shirt. It was so soaked with blood that it was ruined. I burned it. I have some of Thomas's shirts, though, and you can wear one of them. It might not fit perfectly, but he was a good-sized man. Like you."

Blast it, she was looking at his groin again when she said that last, thought Longarm. He understood how she could have gotten mighty randy, being out here on this ranch by herself for the past three years, but couldn't she show a little bit of pity to a wounded man?

Beth fetched the coffeepot and a couple of cups while

Longarm started on the flapjacks and bacon. She was an even better cook than Heck Wallace, he decided. He put away all the food she had brought him, and she returned to the other room for more.

While he was washing the second helpings down with coffee, Beth said, "Don't you think you should tell me what it is you wanted to take from the Wallace gang?"

Longarm hesitated. He remembered the attempts on his life and said, "It might be better for you if you don't know, ma'am." He didn't want her to be drawn any deeper into the case than she already was.

"Then how will I know what to do if somebody shows up looking for you?" she insisted.

"I already told you—turn me over to them."

"I won't do that," she said bluntly.

Longarm sighed in frustration. Yet he could understand how Beth felt. She was trying to nurse him back to health, and she didn't want to see all her hard work go to waste.

"I want to take a look around the ranch," he said after a moment. "Maybe there's someplace you can hide me if you need to."

"All right. Are you sure you're strong enough?"

He grinned. "After everything you've done, Miz Jellicoe, I feel like a new man."

"Call me Beth. And I'm not finished yet."

Now, what did she mean by *that*? Longarm asked himself, then decided that he would find out soon enough.

She brought his clothes into the room, including one of her late husband's shirt. Longarm turned down her offer to help him get dressed, and when he stood up this time, the floor was good and solid under his feet.

He pulled the clothes on, noting that she had washed his trousers and socks and the bottom half of the long underwear he had been wearing. It felt good to stamp his feet down in his boots and buckle his gunbelt around his waist.

He was carrying his hat as he stepped out of the bedroom and got his first look at the rest of the adobe ranch house. It wasn't very big, just one room besides the bedroom, with a fireplace on one wall, a cast-iron stove in the corner, and a big hardwood table in the center of the room. Like the bed, it looked as if it had originally come from much fancier surroundings. He wondered if Beth had belonged to a wealthy Louisiana family before coming out here to West Texas.

She was waiting for him, the broad-brimmed hat he had seen the day before on her head. "How do you feel?" she asked. "Still all right? Not too shaky?"

"Not bad," said Longarm. He settled his hat on his head and stepped out onto a narrow porch with her.

The morning was already warm, with the sun climbing in a cloudless sky. Longarm looked to the right, and saw a good-sized adobe barn with a pole corral behind it. There were more corrals to the left, and in front of him, on the other side of a tiny creek, was a garden. Everything looked to be in good repair, and he supposed he sounded a little dubious as he said to Beth, "You keep all this up by yourself?"

"You think I'm not up to it?" she said.

"That's not it," Longarm assured her. "I just know how much work it takes to run a ranch like this."

"I have a couple of *vaqueros* who work for me," she admitted. "But they stay at a line shack north of here most of the time."

"You and your husband didn't have any children?"

She shook her head. "I . . . lost one the first year. The nearest doctor was down at Fort Stockton then. He told me later that I couldn't have any more." She sounded pretty matter-of-fact about it, but Longarm could hear a faint note of remembered pain and grief in her voice. Some hurts stayed with a person, no matter how much time passed.

"There's a cellar in the barn," Beth went on, sounding more brisk and businesslike now. "Thomas and the hands dug it so we'd have a place to hide in case of cyclones. They can be bad out here, you know."

Longarm nodded. "I've seen a few twisters. A cellar's a good thing to have."

"I store vegetables in it too, and sometimes keep buttermilk there. If those outlaws came, you could hide there."

"They'd be liable to see the trapdoor."

"Not if I covered it with hay after you climbed in," said Beth.

Well, that was possible, thought Longarm. But he still hoped it never came to that. Another day, and he would be ready to travel, he told himself. Enough of his strength would have returned by then to make the ride into Monahans.

He hoped Nora was holding up all right. No matter how crazy she had acted when he tried to help her, he didn't want her coming to any harm at the hands of the outlaws, or anybody else.

Longarm and Beth walked out to the barn, where he checked on the dun. She had obviously rubbed the horse down and made sure it had plenty of grain and water.

"He's an ornery cuss," Longarm told Beth. "I hope he didn't try to nip you while you were fooling with him."

"This horse? Ornery?" She opened the gate and stepped into the stall with the dun. As she began rubbing his nose, she went on. "He's not a bit of trouble."

The dun bobbed his head up and down as if agreeing with her, and Longarm thought the horse had a glint of malicious humor in its eyes. He decided that was carrying things a mite too far and told himself not to think such foolish thoughts.

Beth gave the dun a final pat and then left the stall to lead Longarm to a rear corner of the barn. A platform of heavy planks had been built there, and in the center of it was a trapdoor. Beth bent down and unlatched it, then swung the door up.

Longarm peered down into the cellar and breathed in the musty smell of damp earth. It likely wouldn't be a very pleasant place to hide, and he hoped it wouldn't come to that.

"You see, the hayloft is right above here," Beth pointed

out. "It wouldn't take but a minute to climb up there and fork down enough hay to cover the door."

Longarm nodded. "Likely you won't need to. I'll be riding on to Monahans tomorrow."

She turned to him, clearly surprised. "Tomorrow? You're leaving tomorrow?"

"I gave some thought to riding out today, but I don't reckon I'm quite strong enough for that yet."

"Oh. I suppose . . . you have a job to do. . . ."

"That's right."

She shook her head. "I don't think it's a good idea. You lost too much blood, you're weak."

"The way you've been feeding me, my strength is coming back fast."

She didn't say anything to that, just turned and walked out of the barn. Longarm was afraid he had offended her some way and went after her.

"Miz Jellicoe? Beth?" He caught up to her and put a hand on her arm.

She jerked away from him. "Leave me alone!" she snapped.

Longarm reached out, took hold of her arm again, and turned her to face him. He saw tears sparkling in her eyes.

"Whatever I did to hurt you, Beth, I never meant to," he said sincerely. "I reckon I probably owe you my life. If you hadn't found me and taken care of me—"

"I would have done the same thing for anybody," she bit out. "You don't mean anything special to me, Mr. Long. I never saw you before yesterday, and I'll likely never see you again after you ride away."

Longarm said softly, "Are you trying to convince me, ma'am, or yourself?"

Her right hand came up and flashed toward his face. He caught her wrist before the slap could land. He was holding both of her arms now, and when he pulled her toward him, she didn't resist. Her head tipped back, her eyes closed, and her lips parted slightly as his mouth came down on hers.

This was crazy, he told himself as he kissed her. He was in no shape for romping with any woman, even a beautiful young widow lady like Beth Jellicoe. But as her hands pressed against his chest, her fingers worked with need and desire. Her tongue thrust boldly into his mouth. It had been a long time for her, much too long.

When they broke the kiss after a lengthy, sensuous moment, Beth whispered, "Mr. Long . . ."

"Custis," he told her.

"Custis. I know I have no . . . no right to ask, but . . . come in the house with me."

Longarm rested a hand under her jaw, gently stroking the length of it and on down to her neck. "I still have to ride on tomorrow," he told her.

"I know. But . . . tomorrow is a long time off. . . ."

Not long enough, thought Longarm. However long this day was, it wouldn't be enough.

She led him to the house, holding his hand almost like a shy little girl. They went to the bedroom, and Beth began to undress. She tossed the broad-brimmed hat aside and then her fingers went to the buttons of her dress. She unfastened them quickly, no awkwardness or fumbling about her movements. She knew what she wanted, and she was determined to have it. The dress fell around her feet, followed a moment later by the shift she wore under it. She stepped out of the clothes, wearing only high-button shoes and stockings. Longarm's gaze traveled over her appreciatively, noting the full breasts crowned with large, dark brown nipples, the slightly rounded belly above the thick triangle of dark hair, the smooth-skinned curves of hips and thighs. She was every bit as beautiful as he had known she would be.

"Now you," she whispered, tugging at the shirt that had once belonged to her husband.

She wanted to undress him, so Longarm obliged her. He was already erect, so that when she knelt in front of him to pull down his long underwear, his shaft sprang free and nearly hit her in the eye. Smiling, she caught hold of it and held it as she rubbed her cheek against the head. Her fingers were not quite long enough to completely encircle the thick pole of male flesh.

"Sit down," she said. "I'll take your boots off."

He had quite a compelling view as she turned her back to him and bent over to take first one boot off for him, then the other. The sight of her bottom, full and rounded, with the darker cleft that divided it, made him throb with anticipation.

When he was as naked as she was except for the bandages, she put her hands on his chest and pressed him down on the bed. "Let me do all the work," she said. "You still need your rest."

Longarm had serious doubts about how restful this was going to be, but he nodded his agreement.

She knelt between his legs and lowered her head. He thought she was going to take his shaft in her mouth, but instead she grasped it in her hand at the base and just sort of . . . looked at it . . . for a while. The expression on her face was that of someone gazing at something they had been missing for a long, long time, only to find it again unexpectedly. He hadn't known how maddening it could be for a woman to just study him that way. When Beth's tongue came out and licked over her lips, he almost shot off then and there.

She reached down and cupped his sac, rolling the male orbs back and forth. Then she slid her fingers up and around his shaft, tracing practically every inch of it. She closed both hands around him, obviously relishing the hot, thick feel of him. Then she leaned forward again, tongue protruding slightly between her lips, and began giving him tiny licks that were as light as a butterfly landing on a flower.

After only a couple of those, Longarm came like Old Faithful.

She must have felt his climax boiling up, because she opened her mouth wider and engulfed him just before his seed began to erupt. The muscles in her throat worked as she took what he gave her. She caught hold of his balls again and squeezed lightly, as if she wanted to make sure she was milking him dry. Longarm's hips came up off the bed as he jetted spurt after scalding spurt into her mouth.

He fell back after what seemed like an eternity. His chest rose and fell quickly as he tried to catch his breath. Beth still knelt between his legs with his shaft cradled in her mouth. Longarm should have been going soft right about now.

He realized he wasn't. He still wanted her as badly as she wanted him.

She gave his manhood a last lick and kiss, then slid up his body, being careful not to put any weight on his injured side. A broad smile was on her face as she straddled his hips, caught hold of his shaft, and lowered herself onto it. Her mouth opened and her eyes closed as he slid into her. Her bottom bumped against his thighs. He was in her all the way, had penetrated as deeply as he could go. Beth sighed as her hips began to pump back and forth.

"Let me know . . . if I hurt you," she whispered without opening her eyes.

"That ain't . . . very likely," gasped Longarm.

She truly did all the work. He lay there and enjoyed it as her body stroked his again and again. For a few minutes, he caressed her thighs, then lifted his hands to her breasts, cupping and squeezing the mounds of soft flesh. His thumbs strummed her nipples, which were hard and pebbled with need.

Longarm's first climax insured that he didn't come too soon this time. In fact, it felt as if they had been screwing for hours when he finally erupted again, just as Beth's own spasms were shaking her like a sapling in a stiff wind. Or one of those cyclones she had mentioned earlier, he thought. Their shared climax was so shattering, they might as well have been caught up in a twister.

Then, just as if they had indeed been snatched up off the earth by forces of nature, they came spiraling back down, only their landing was soft and hot and filled with whispered words and passionate kisses. Longarm held her close and thought how lucky he had been to emerge from the sand hills at just the right spot to run into her.

Lucky, of course, assuming she didn't love him to death before he got a chance to ride away from there. . . .

Chapter 16

It was hoofbeats and the clinking of spurs and saddle harness that woke Longarm.

He and Beth had both dozed off sometime during the afternoon, sated and exhausted by their lovemaking. Now, as warning sounds drifted in through the window, Longarm's eyes snapped open and his hand shot out to close around the butt of the Colt. Out of habit, he had left the cross-draw rig hanging on one of the bedposts, close at hand. As he snagged the gun, he rolled out of bed, landing lightly on the floor in a crouch.

Beth sat up sharply, disturbed by his sudden movements. "What—"

Longarm held his left index finger to his mouth and hissed softly at her. A moment later, a man's voice called, "Hello, the house?"

Longarm frowned. He didn't recognize the voice. It certainly wasn't the rasping growl of Heck Wallace, nor the drawl of Van Horn or the good-natured tones of Dutchy. In fact, Longarm was convinced it didn't belong to any of the outlaws, not even the taciturn Funderburk.

Who? Longarm mouthed at Beth. She just shook her head, clearly as puzzled as he was.

"Anybody home?"

Beth swung her legs out of bed and reached for her dress. "Just a minute!" she called, ignoring Longarm's gestures instructing her to be quiet.

Well, that tore it, thought Longarm with a grimace. Whoever it was out there, now Beth would have to deal with them. There had been a chance that if no one responded, the visitors would just go away.

But not a very good chance, Longarm admitted to himself. Maybe Beth had done the right thing. For all he knew, the strangers could be lawmen, maybe even members of the posse that had tried to ambush the Wallace gang a couple of days earlier. Longarm's troubles might be over.

Then again . . .

Hurriedly, he pulled his pants on. A man didn't feel quite so defenseless if he wasn't naked. Beth was buttoning up her dress as the man called again from out front. "Ma'am?"

"I'll be right there," Beth replied, raising her voice so that he could hear her. She glanced at Longarm, and he motioned with the barrel of the Colt for her to go ahead.

She went out of the bedroom, leaving the door slightly ajar behind her. Longarm pressed his eye to the crack and watched as she went to the door of the ranch house and opened it to step out onto the porch. She left that door wide open so that he could see what was happening. She was a fast thinker, Longarm had to give her that. With the late afternoon sun so bright outside, the visitors wouldn't be able to see very well into the house.

"Hello," said Beth, her voice loud enough so that Longarm could hear her plainly. "What can I do for you gentlemen?"

Smart, thought Longarm. She had just warned him that there was more than one of them.

A man on horseback edged into Longarm's field of view. He reached up and tugged on the wide brim of his hat as he said, "Howdy, ma'am. Sorry to bother you. We just wanted to know if we could water our horses at your well."

"Of course," said Beth, sounding pleasant and hospitable. "Help yourself."

"Much obliged." The man swung his horse a little.

Longarm saw the butt of a Spencer carbine sticking up from a saddle boot.

He knew that hat too, he thought as his breath caught in his throat. This time he wasn't mistaken. This man was the one who had bushwhacked him up in New Mexico Territory. Longarm was sure of it. The fella wasn't wearing a duster now, but that was because it was too hot for one down here in West Texas.

So the would-be killer had trailed him from Ashcroft after all, Longarm mused. And he wasn't alone either. He had brought more gunmen with him. As the riders milled around, letting their horses drink from the well in front of the ranch house, Longarm caught glimpses of at least four different men. From the sound of their horses, there could have been even more.

Longarm could see Beth standing there on the porch, arms folded, watching coolly as the visitors watered their mounts. The leader, the fella with the Spencer, walked his horse back up to the porch again and said, "Thank you, ma'am."

"You're welcome," Beth returned.

"By the way, you wouldn't happen to have seen a stranger around here in the past day or two, would you?"

"No, I don't think so," said Beth, answering with the quickness of confidence in her reply, but not too quickly.

"Big, broad-shouldered fellow with a longhorn mustache?"

"No, I told you I haven't seen any strangers. And I don't mix in other people's business either."

"That's always a wise course to take. I just wanted to warn you about this man. He's a criminal, a cold-blooded murderer. We've been hunting him for a week now."

"You're lawmen?" asked Beth.

"Bounty hunters."

"Does this man you're looking for have a name?"

134

"He's calling himself Custis Long," said the man with the Spencer. "But that's not his real name. He killed a U.S. deputy marshal up in Colorado and took the deputy's badge and identification papers. He's been passing himself off as Long ever since."

Longarm tensed. That was a damned clever story, and he watched closely to see how Beth reacted to it.

"That's terrible," she said without missing a beat. "I hope you find him."

The man touched the brim of his hat again. "Oh, we will, I can promise you that. Thanks again for the water, ma'am, and you'd better keep an eye out for that killer."

"I will," Beth said.

A moment later, the men rode off. Beth stayed on the porch for a minute, watching them leave, then turned and came back into the house. "They're gone, Custis," she said.

He stepped out of the bedroom, his eyes searching her face. "That son of a buck was lying to you," he said. "I really am Custis Long. That fella took a shot at me up in New Mexico Territory a few days ago, and I reckon he's been hoping for another chance ever since."

"I believe you," she said. "Maybe it's foolish of me, but I just don't believe that a man as . . . as gentle as you could be a cold-blooded killer."

Longarm lowered the hammer of the Colt. "I'd be hard-pressed not to take a shot at that gent if I got the chance," he admitted. "But I really am a deputy marshal."

"I believe that too."

"Which way did they go?"

"They rode southeast, toward Monahans."

He nodded. "Then I reckon that's where I'm going too."

She stepped closer, lifted a hand as if she was about to touch his arm, then hesitated. "I thought you weren't leaving until tomorrow."

"The reason that fella wants me dead has to have something to do with the job that brought me down here. It's time I found out what, and maybe if I can catch up to them in

Monahans, I can learn what I need to know."

"But you're still recovering from that gunshot wound," she protested. "You said yourself you were too weak to ride that far. . . ."

"I'll be all right," he told her. "I can't afford to pass up this chance, Beth." He turned and started into the bedroom to get dressed.

Beth was silent for a moment. Then she said, "I've got an extra saddle. I'll go put it on that dun for you."

She was an unusual woman, all right, thought Longarm. Even though he had only known her for a couple of days, he was going to miss her.

Maybe he could get back this way someday—after he found out what the hell was going on with Nora Canady and why that fella with the Spencer carbine wanted him dead.

Beth was an observant woman. She was able to tell Longarm that there had been six men in the group altogether. She described them—hardcases every one, from the sound of it— as well as their horses. Longarm was certain he would be able to recognize the men when he found them.

But unless he saw them first, they were likely to recognize him too, and that would lead to shooting. That wasn't what Longarm wanted. He needed to know who had sent these hired killers after him. As far as he could see, there were still only a couple of possibilities.

"Be careful," Beth murmured as he was ready to mount up.

"I intend to be," he promised her.

"Any time you're back in these parts . . ."

"I'll stop. You've got my word on it. But, Beth . . . maybe you better not count on me ever being back this way. Might be a good idea for you to find somebody else. It's a mighty lonely life out here for a woman."

A bittersweet smile curved her lips. "I've known two good men in my life. Who knows? Maybe another one will come along someday."

Longarm bent to brush his lips over hers. "I hope so," he said.

Then, before he could regret it even more, he swung up into the saddle and heeled the dun into a trot that carried him away from the ranch—and the woman who lived there.

The men hadn't made any effort to cover their trail. Longarm followed it easily. They were cutting across country, not bothering to take the stage road, which ran to the west. It didn't really matter. In this flat, mostly barren country, one place was as easy to ride as another.

The sun was halfway below the horizon to the west when Longarm came in sight of Monahans. The sand hills were visible to the east, and it looked like the town was situated at the southern end of the dunes. Monahans wasn't a very old town, he reflected. This was the route the Texas & Pacific Railroad would take as it was built across West Texas, but the iron rails weren't here yet. Monahans was ready, though, for when the railhead arrived. He saw plenty of lights blazing in the gathering dusk, and when he got closer to the settlement, he could hear tinny piano music floating on the evening air. The saloons were already doing a good business just from the ranches in the area, Longarm speculated. When the railroad arrived, the place would really boom.

He swung wide to the west to avoid entering the town by its main street. Under the circumstances, with those hired guns around, it would be foolish, maybe even fatal, to ride in right out in the open. Instead he found a back alley that ran behind some of the false-fronted buildings and eased the dun along it. He dismounted and tied the horse to a greasewood bush behind a building that was probably a general store, judging from the jumble of empty crates just outside the rear door.

The sun had set now, and night was falling rapidly. Longarm sidled along a narrow passage between buildings. It was dark and shadowy there, and he was able to reach the street without anyone noticing him. He stood there, just inside the mouth of the little gap, and let his gaze range up and down the street, checking out the horses tied at all the hitch racks he could see.

It took him only a moment to spot six tied together in front of a saloon called the Sure Shot. He wondered if Cap'n Billy knew about that. Probably not. The owner of the place had to be well-to-do; the building had two actual stories, instead of one real one and a false front. A flight of stairs ran up the side of the building to a door that opened onto the second floor. That seemed a likely way to get inside, so Longarm faded back into the passageway and returned to the alley. He went along it to the end of the block, then circled the last building and walked quickly across the street, keeping his head down so that his Stetson concealed part of his face. Again, no one seemed to pay any attention to him, although the street was busy with wagon and horse traffic and the boardwalks were crowded with pedestrians.

Longarm catfooted through more alleys, and wound up in the passage between the saloon and its neighboring building, a saddle shop that was closed for the night. He walked to the bottom of the outside stairs and swung onto them, climbing briskly as if he belonged there and knew exactly what he was doing. He would look a little foolish if he got to the top and the door was locked, he thought.

Luck was with him. The door swung open as soon as he turned the knob. He stepped into a deserted corridor that was dimly lit by a lamp at the far end. There were doors along the hallway, all of them closed at the moment. Those rooms were no doubt where the girls who worked in the saloon conducted their real business, so he couldn't count on the hall staying empty for long. At any second, one of the gals could drag some young cowboy up there for a few minutes of bought-and-paid-for pleasure.

Longarm walked swiftly and silently down the corridor. It opened onto a landing at the far end, and there was also a short, railed balcony that overlooked the saloon's main room. He stopped when he reached the balcony and edged an eye past the corner. He could see the long, polished bar from there, and he spotted five men standing together, propping their heels on the brass rail as they nursed beers. He recognized them from Beth's description.

But there were only five of them. The man in the broad-brimmed hat, the man who carried a Spencer carbine, wasn't with them.

His horse was tied up outside, which meant he was in here somewhere. In one of the rooms maybe, with one of the saloon girls. Longarm couldn't bust into every one with his gun drawn until he found the man he wanted, though he considered the idea for a second. That would raise too much of a ruckus and attract the attention of the gunmen downstairs. Nor could he just stand there and wait, because someone was bound to come along pretty soon—

A door opened somewhere along the corridor behind him.

There was no time for any but the simplest plan. Longarm turned, lowered his head, and started walking unsteadily along the corridor toward the door that opened onto the outside stairs. If the person who was stepping out into the hall was anybody other than the hired killer with the Spencer, they would probably just take him for a drunk and not pay much attention to him. That was what he was hoping anyway.

"I'll be right back, sweetheart," he heard a woman say, and a shock ran through him as he realized that her voice was somehow familiar. "You and Mr. Carter go ahead with your business."

"All right, but don't be long," a man told her. His voice was curt, businesslike, clearly accustomed to command. It was deep and rich, an orator's voice.

Longarm knew it too.

It belonged to Senator Jonas Palmer.

And as Longarm lifted his eyes to the woman who was walking along the hallway toward him, he saw a familiar face to go along with her voice. Her eyes widened as she recognized him just as he had recognized her. Her mouth opened wide too, and Longarm knew that in another second, a scream would be coming out of it.

He lunged forward and clapped a hand over her mouth, at the same time looping his other arm around her waist. He jerked her against him, turning her so that her back came up solidly against his chest. He pinned her there so that she couldn't move, and kept his hand over her mouth so tightly that not even a squawk could escape.

"Well, if it ain't Miss Emily Toplin," he hissed in her ear. "I never expected to run into you down here in Texas. Tried to stab anybody lately?"

Chapter 17

The young woman tried to struggle, but Longarm held her too tightly for her to do anything except squirm a little. He backed toward the door at the far end of the corridor. Trapped in his grip, Emily had no choice but to go with him.

Longarm reached the door and realized he was faced with a dilemma. If he took his hand away from Emily's mouth, she would scream. If he let go of her with his other arm, she would try to break away from him and might be able to do it. But he had to get the door open somehow, and quietly too.

So he did the only thing he could, even though he didn't like it. He whirled Emily around unexpectedly, taking her by surprise, and snatched his hand away from her mouth long enough to ball it loosely into a fist and clip her on the jaw with it.

Her head lolled back and she sagged toward him, stunned by the blow. Longarm caught her.

If he hadn't been recuperating from a gunshot wound, he probably would have just slung her over his shoulder and carried her out of the saloon. He wasn't sure he could do that without causing his wound to start bleeding again, so he settled for wrapping an arm around her again and half-dragging, half-carrying her through the door and down the outside stairs. A couple of times, he thought he was going to lose his balance and topple the rest of the way, taking Emily with him, but he managed to stay upright. When he reached the bottom of the stairs, he was confident that anyone who had observed their lurching descent would just assume that both he and the woman with him were drunk.

He turned and took Emily down the shadow-cloaked passage between the buildings. She was regaining her senses by now, shaking her head and muttering, and she tried to pull away from the hand that he had clamped on her arm.

"Settle down," Longarm told her. "I don't like hitting women, but it don't bother me near as much when they've tried to kill me."

"You . . . how did you . . . where . . . damn you."

Well, that last part was coherent enough, he thought wryly.

"How'd I find you and Palmer?" asked Longarm. "Simple enough. I followed the fella who's been following me. You called him Carter. Wouldn't be Simeon Carter, now would it?"

Longarm had recalled that name from a wanted poster he'd seen. Simeon Carter was a hired killer, a former Union officer during the Civil War, who was wanted in Montana for his activities as a regulator during a bloody range feud. Longarm had never seen a picture of him, but he was willing to bet the man with the Spencer carbine was indeed Carter.

"Go to Hell," Emily said thickly.

"Is that any way for a gal who looks like she just came from prayer meeting to talk?"

She gave him an even more obscene, not to mention physically impossible, suggestion.

Longarm reached the alley behind the Sure Shot. He pushed Emily up against the wall of the building, not hard but firmly enough to let her know that he didn't intend to let her get away.

"You're under arrest for the attempted murder of a federal officer," he told her. "That's the very least that's going to happen to you. But it could get worse if you don't tell me

142

what you know about Palmer and Carter and why they want me dead.''

"I'm not going to tell you a damned thing.''

"You looking forward to spending the next twenty years behind bars, Emily? You won't be a fresh-faced gal when you get out of prison.''

He couldn't see her face very well in the gloom of the alley, but he could feel the tension in her body as he held her arms. She cursed at him again.

"Been called worse,'' he said calmly. "That don't change anything.'' He paused, then said, "Palmer's your lover, isn't he?''

"What if he is?'' Emily shot back.

"You probably didn't cotton much to the idea of him marrying Nora Canady, did you? But he was going to go through with the wedding anyway, because her father's a mighty rich man. What was Palmer going to do after that, Emily, keep you as his mistress? His whore?''

"You shut up,'' she hissed. "You just shut up. You don't know anything about it.''

"Then why don't you tell me?''

"He's going to miss me, you know. I was just going downstairs to get another bottle of brandy. When I don't come back, Jonas will come looking for me.''

"By then you'll already be in jail. You'll never see Palmer again unless it's at your trial.'' Longarm laughed humorlessly. "And he probably won't come. He won't even admit that he knows you.''

"You're crazy!''

"Nope, just practical. The senator's not going to want to have anything to do with a gal who's on trial for attempted murder. Not when he's married to somebody like Nora.''

"He'll never be married to her!'' Emily blazed at him. "I told you you don't know what you're talking about. She'll be dead!''

"Because Palmer wants her dead,'' Longarm said quietly, putting some of the pieces together in his mind. "He didn't

143

want me to look for her in the first place. Canady must have insisted that they bring in the Justice Department, and Palmer didn't have any choice but to go along with him. But then he sent you after me to make sure I didn't find Nora. When that didn't work, he hired Carter.''

''You think you're so damned smart.''

''Smart enough to figure out that after Carter killed me, he was supposed to eliminate Nora too. That's why you said the senator would never marry her. Why would Palmer want to kill the woman he was supposed to marry?''

Emily said, ''I'm not going to tell you anything else, you bastard. You don't stand a chance against Jonas. He's smarter than you.''

''Maybe so, but I'm still loose, and he can't be happy about that.'' Longarm let go of her with one hand and reached into his pocket for his bandanna. ''Open your mouth.''

''The hell with that! You can go—''

He didn't want to listen to that downright unlikely suggestion again, so while her jaw was flapping angrily, he shoved the balled bandanna into her mouth. While she tried unsuccessfully to spit it out, he hooked a foot behind her legs and pulled them out from under her. Emily sat down hard on the floor of the alley.

Longarm ripped a strip off the hem of her dress and used it to tie the gag in place, then tore another strip to bind her wrists behind her. Emily struggled all the time he was doing that, so he was a little breathless by the time he got through tying her feet together with another strip of fabric.

He dragged her over to a clump of mesquite trees behind the buildings. ''You'll be all right here for a while,'' he told her. ''There's supposed to a sheriff in this town, but even if there is, I ain't got time to roust him out. Just lay there and be quiet. Somebody's bound to be along directly.''

She made furious, muffled noises at him.

''Sorry to have to treat you so bad. But you shouldn't have tried to stick that knife between my ribs neither.''

He left her under the trees and returned to the narrow passage beside the saloon. Staying near the wall so the stairs wouldn't creak, he climbed swiftly to the second floor and eased the door open a fraction of an inch.

Emily had been right about one thing: Palmer had expected her to return before now. In fact, the senator was standing in the corridor, and he sounded downright worried as he said, "Forget about Long for now, Carter. See if you can find Emily."

The hired killer was standing with Palmer just outside the door of the senator's room. He nodded and said, "I'll check downstairs. That was where she was going."

"I know that, damn it," snapped Palmer. Longarm watched as Palmer rubbed a weary hand over his face. "I can't afford to have the wrong people get their hands on her. She knows too much about my deal with Canady."

Longarm stiffened. That told him a little more about Palmer's reasons for wanting his fiancée dead, but it raised even more questions. Bryce Canady was in on this too? It sure sounded that way.

But Longarm had a hard time reconciling that theory with the worry, the outright fear, he had seen on Canady's face there in Billy Vail's office. Canady had seemed genuinely mystified about his daughter's disappearance, and Longarm would have bet money on the fact that all Canady wanted was Nora's safe return.

Well, he'd have to puzzle that out later, Longarm told himself. He waited until Carter had gone downstairs and Palmer had stepped back into the room. Then he opened the door the rest of the way and moved into the corridor. He drew his gun as he went to the senator's room and knocked sharply on the door.

Palmer yanked it open a second later, saying, "That was fast—"

He stopped in mid-sentence as Longarm dug the barrel of the Colt into the soft flesh under his chin.

145

"Howdy, Senator," Longarm said quietly. "I reckon you didn't expect to see me."

Palmer started making little noises, and Longarm knew he was about to yell. Longarm pressed harder on Palmer's throat with the gun and shook his head.

"Wouldn't do that if I was you. I'm feeling a mite perturbed right about now, Senator. Come to find out you never wanted me to find Miss Canady after all. You just wanted me dead."

With the pressure of the gun, Longarm forced Palmer backward several steps. Longarm used the heel of his boot to kick the door closed behind them. A glance around the room told him that he and Palmer were alone.

But for how long?

"Marshal Long," Palmer grated between clenched teeth, "what the hell are you doing?"

"Talking to a low-down, double-crossing skunk," said Longarm.

Despite the situation, a smile stretched across Palmer's face. "I've served in the United States Senate for seven years, Long. You're going to have to do better than that if you want to insult me."

Longarm felt like pistol-whipping the son of a bitch, but he controlled the impulse. "Why'd you send Carter after me?" he asked. "What is it you're trying to hide, Senator?"

"I don't know what you're talking about. And I'm going to have your badge for assaulting me, Long!"

"Go right ahead and try to have me fired, mister. We'll see how far you get once that lady friend of yours who just left here is done talking."

That got the reaction Longarm had hoped for. Palmer's eyes narrowed, and he said angrily, "Emily? You have Emily?"

"Yep. And she was right eager to talk, once I explained to her how long she'd have to go to prison for trying to murder a federal officer. She said you put her up to it, just like you hired Carter to kill me later on. And she told me

146

how you planned to have Carter kill Miss Canady too, once he caught up to her."

"Emily wouldn't talk to you," Palmer said with a sneer, but Longarm heard a faint quiver of uncertainty in his voice.

"Maybe you should have thought about how it would make her feel to share your bed and do your dirty work, when all the while you were planning to marry another woman."

Palmer blinked rapidly, nervousness now visible on his face. Longarm had played two opponents against each other before, and it usually worked. He could only hope that it would in this case too.

"Emily doesn't know nearly as much as she thinks she does," blustered Palmer.

"Enough to ruin your career and put you behind bars." Longarm paused and then added meaningfully, "Unless it was all Canady's idea."

"Bryce? He wouldn't—"

Palmer stopped abruptly, realizing that he had almost revealed too much. What he had said made Longarm believe that Canady hadn't known anything about Carter's involvement. The railroad baron might be up to something no good with Palmer, but at least his concern for his daughter had been genuine.

"So you hired Carter on your own," Longarm said. "That means you're the only one who wants Miss Nora dead. That's mighty interesting, considering that you were supposed to be married to her by now."

"I would have been too," Palmer practically spat. "None of this would have happened if she hadn't—"

A heavy knock sounded on the door.

Longarm reached for Palmer's shoulder, intending to haul the senator around in front of him to use as a shield just in case Carter came busting in that door, but Palmer surprised him. Disregarding for the moment his own personal safety, Palmer lashed out, aiming a kick at Longarm's groin. Longarm was forced to twist in order to take the kick on his thigh, and that pulled the gun away from Palmer's neck long enough for the politician to grab Longarm's wrist. "Carter!" Palmer shouted. "Get in here!"

Longarm didn't bother trying to jerk the wrist of his gun hand out of Palmer's grip. He swung his left fist instead, smashing it into Palmer's midsection, then backhanded the senator when Palmer doubled over in pain. That knocked Palmer loose from Longarm's gun hand.

Pivoting smoothly toward the door, Longarm was ready when Carter kicked it open. Carter had to hesitate, to make sure that Palmer wasn't in the line of fire before he started shooting. Longarm didn't have to wait. He triggered two shots toward the opening as soon as the door flew back.

Carter went diving to the side, and Longarm didn't know if he had hit the man or not. He turned, slashing at Palmer with the Colt as he did so. The barrel raked across Palmer's face, the sight opening a nasty gash in his cheek. Palmer flew backward, leaving Longarm with an open path to the room's single window.

That was one hell of a way to leave the room, but Longarm didn't see anything else he could do. Carter was in the hall, and the other five hired killers were downstairs. Longarm took a couple of steps and then lunged, ducking his head to protect his face from flying glass as he crashed out through the window, taking its flimsy frame with him.

There was no balcony outside the window, but there was a roof over the boardwalk in front of the saloon. Longarm had noticed it earlier. He fell only about four feet before he hit the slightly sloping roof. He rolled over once, caught himself, and threw a shot in the busted-out window to discourage Palmer and Carter from using it to fire at him. He kept rolling and dropped off the edge of the roof.

This fall was a little farther, a good ten feet to the street. Longarm landed on his boots and went down into a crouch, but he managed not to fall over. Pain shot through his side at the impact, and he was sure he had torn the wound open again. He couldn't worry about that now. Carter's men would be rushing upstairs to see what was happening, but it wouldn't take them long to realize he had gone out through the window. Already, he could hear Carter shouting, "Downstairs! He's down in the street, you idiots!"

Longarm broke into a run that carried him across the street. He couldn't go back for Emily, couldn't do anything except get to the dun and ride out of Monahans as fast as possible.

He was limping a little as he hurried down the alley next to a building that housed a general mercantile. He thought he had the right place, and sure enough, when he emerged into the rear alley, he spotted the dun in the moonlight. The horse was still tied to the greasewood tree. Longarm grabbed the reins, jerked them loose, and swung up into the saddle with no regard for the small but spreading patch of wetness on his side. The blood from the wound must have already started soaking through the bandages Beth had tied tightly around him.

He kicked the dun into a gallop. The running hoofbeats would be plainly audible in the night. Carter and the rest of the hired guns could follow him by sound alone if they got a quick start.

That was all right with Longarm. The wound in his side ached, and his leg had been hurt a little in the fall from the roof, but there was nothing wrong with his brain.

And he had an idea about how he might be able to settle this whole mess, once and for all.

Provided nobody killed him first, of course . . .

Chapter 18

Longarm circled Monahans and rode north, skirting the western edge of the sand hills. He probably could have lost the pursuit by entering the dunes, but that wasn't what he wanted. The way he saw it, his best chance to settle everything depended on Carter's men being able to follow him.

His plan was dangerous, especially for Nora Canady, but there was no way to keep her out of danger now. He had already tried once to get her away from the Wallace gang, and all that had gotten him was a hot lead furrow plowed in his side. Nora would just have to take her chances.

Besides, if he could get his hands on her again, she might be more reasonable this time, since he now knew that her prospective bridegroom wanted to kill her. Nora must have known that too, and that was why she had left Denver and taken off for the tall and uncut. If Longarm could get her away from the outlaws and convince her that he wouldn't be taking her back to her death, maybe he could find out *why* it was so important to Palmer to get rid of her. It was something to do with some deal Palmer had with Bryce Canady, Longarm knew that much. . . .

He was glad the dun had had a chance to rest at Beth Jellicoe's ranch. He called on the horse now for all the strength and stamina it possessed. A glance over his shoulder showed Longarm the lights of Monahans receding in the distance to the south. A haze of dust hung in the air between Longarm and the settlement, vaguely visible in the starlight. That would be the dust from the horses of Carter and his men, thought Longarm. The hired killers were after him, all right.

That was just what he wanted.

He rode steadily on through the night, keeping the dun moving at a good pace. The bleeding in Longarm's side had stopped. At least, the wet place on his shirt was no longer getting any larger. The place hurt, but not more than he could bear.

The moon and stars wheeled through the black velvet sky, revealing the passage of time to Longarm. He kept the sand hills a couple of hundred yards off to his right, watching the terrain carefully. Not that there was much variation in it. The landscape was mostly flat and dotted with sparse vegetation. But there were a few landmarks, and Longarm took note of them, watching for particular ones.

It was well after midnight and the horse was beginning to tire when Longarm spotted a dune that stuck up particularly sharply on the very edge of the sand hills. The dune was topped by a dead, twisted bush. Longarm had seen that bush a couple of days earlier when he'd ridden out of the sand hills, just before his encounter with Beth Jellicoe, whom he had mistaken for Simeon Carter. He would never make that mistake again, hat or no hat, he told himself. Beth was a whole hell of a lot prettier.

He swung the dun toward the sand hills. This was where he had left them, and this was where he would enter them again. He thought he could find the place where the Wallace gang had been camped. Of course, it was likely the campsite had been moved, and the dunes themselves had had time to shift a little, so he might just get lost and wander around in the dunes until his bones joined all the others bleaching in the Texas sun.

That was a chance he had to take.

• • •

Dawn found Longarm riding deep in the sand hills. He could no longer be sure that Carter and the other hired killers were on his trail. He wasn't trying to hide his tracks, though, and anyway, that was almost impossible in the sand. Unless they had gone blind, they should have been able to follow him, even by moonlight.

The dun was played out, and so was Longarm. He wanted to curl up somewhere and sleep for about a month. His stomach growled from hunger. He hadn't realized he would miss Beth's cooking so much. Shoot, right about now he even missed Heck Wallace's cooking.

Wallace had been hiding from the law in these sand hills for months now, and Longarm knew it was sheer gail for him to think that he could find the outlaw camp. But on the other hand, he had been a member of the gang, if only for a little while, and he figured he knew more about how Wallace thought than the other star packers who had been searching for him. He knew that Wallace liked to keep to the low ground between dunes. That was where the shin oaks grew, where water could be found, where a fire could not be seen.

All Longarm had to do was cover about four hundred square miles of sand hills.

Not that much, really, he told himself. He knew that Wallace could be found here deep in the interior of the sand hills; the outlaw leader wouldn't camp near the edges of the dunes. Still, it was pretty close to needle-in-a-haystack time again, just as it had been when he'd first started searching for Nora Canady.

He had found Nora then; he could find her—and the Wallace gang—again now.

With that confidence spurring him on, Longarm rode deeper into the rolling hills. The sky grew brighter as the sun rose, and suddenly, off to his left, Longarm spotted something. It was faint, more of a wavering streak of gray against the lightening blue than a column of smoke, but Longarm recognized it anyway. The shin oak the outlaws used for firewood didn't produce much smoke, but it had to smoke a little.

Longarm hoped that was what he was seeing now. He turned the weary dun in that direction and urged the horse on. A few minutes later, the faint tendril of smoke disappeared. Someone had probably put out the fire. That didn't matter. Longarm already had the place pinpointed in his mind.

Distances were tricky here in the sand hills, though, so he was extra careful each time he topped a dune. He didn't want to ride right into plain sight of the outlaws without meaning to. When his instincts told him he was close to the camp, he dismounted and led the dun on foot. He took to crawling up to the top of each dune, taking off his hat, and sneaking a glance over the top before he went on.

Finally, he was rewarded with what he had wanted to see: a camp much like the one the Wallace gang had been using before, in the bottom of a valley between two large dunes. The same sort of makeshift corral had been fashioned by stringing ropes between shin oaks, and all of the gang's horses were in it. Longarm counted them quickly to make sure of that fact. No outrider was on duty at the moment, probably because Wallace was confident that no one could find them.

He hadn't counted on Longarm.

The big lawman's eyes searched for Nora Canady. He saw her sitting on a bedroll, wearing the same dress she had been wearing a couple of days earlier. Her honey-blond hair was in more disarray now, but she seemed to be all right. As Longarm watched, Dutchy brought her a cup of coffee.

Longarm wondered if Van Horn had gone into Monahans to send that ransom letter to Bryce Canady yet. It didn't really matter one way or the other, he told himself. He planned to have Nora out of the hands of the owlhoots long before her father could pay any ransom for her.

He slid down the dune a little, so that he could no longer see the outlaw camp. Rolling onto his back, he sat up and peered back the way he had come. After a few minutes of looking intently out over the sea of sand, Longarm spotted movement. Probably three quarters of a mile behind him, several riders topped a rise for a second before dropping back down out of sight.

A bleak smile stretched Longarm's cracked lips. That would be Carter and the other hired gunmen, following his trail.

Now all he had to do was wait, but that wasn't as easy as it sounded. The minutes dragged by. The sun was well above the horizon by now, and its heat was growing. Longarm took off his hat, sleeved sweat from his face. The wound in his side alternated between aching like the devil and itching like blazes. He wished he had a drink.

The riders came on behind him. He caught another glimpse of them, then another. At long last, he saw them topping a dune only a couple of hundred yards away.

That ought to be just about close enough, he decided.

He stood up and went to the dun, which had been standing with its head down. The horse was about as tired as he was. But as Longarm swung up into the saddle, the dun lifted its head and gave it a defiant toss, as if saying that he could keep going just as long as Longarm could. Longarm patted the animal on the shoulder and said, "Won't be much longer now, old son. You'll be back in a nice comfortable stall before you know it, with plenty of water and all the grain you can eat."

Actually, if everything went according to plan, the horse still had a long, hard run in front of it. But the encouraging words made Longarm feel a little better too.

He drew his Colt, then took a deep breath, and dug his heels into the dun's flanks. The horse lunged forward into a gallop that carried it awkwardly over the top of the sand dune. Longarm let out a whoop and fired a couple of shots, aiming well over the heads of the men in the camp below.

That got the reaction he expected. The men who had been lazing around a moment earlier were now galvanized into

154

action. They leaped to their feet, grabbed their guns, ran for their horses. Gunfire began to bang out. The range was pretty far for accurate shooting with a handgun, however. Longarm saw several puffs of sands where bullets plowed into the hill well ahead of him.

He rode only a few yards down the hill before he reined in the dun and wheeled it around in a tight turn. Then he kicked it into a run again that carried horse and rider back over the crest of the dune. Shots still rang out behind him.

Longarm turned the horse sharply to the right and rode hard in that direction, slanting down the slope.

He hoped the outlaws would come after him, hoped as well that Carter and the other hired guns would come rushing on when they heard the shots. That would put the two groups on a collision course. But Longarm couldn't see either bunch at the moment, so hoping was all he could do.

Then, as he reached the bottom of the depression between the two long ridges of sand, all hell broke loose behind him.

Longarm slowed the dun and twisted in the saddle. He saw that the Wallace gang and Carter's bunch had topped the hills opposite each other at almost the same moment. Longarm grinned at how well the timing had worked out. Each group of gunmen, seeing a bunch of strangers coming at them, had acted on instinct and started blazing away at each other. Longarm saw several men go flying from their saddles.

He turned the dun yet again and started climbing back up the sand hill as the battle raged a few hundred yards to his right. He had to move fast, because there was always the possibility that the desperadoes and the hired killers wouldn't wipe each other out. Any survivors might figure out what he had done, and then they would head for the outlaw camp as fast as they could.

The horse reached the top of the slope and surged over it. Longarm veered toward the camp, and as he did, a rifle cracked and a slug whined past his ear. He leaned forward over the neck of the dun and saw that Heck Wallace was still at the camp, guarding Nora. Longarm had hoped that Wallace would join the headlong charge, but the outlaw leader was too wily to be drawn in. Now Longarm had to meet him head-on if he wanted to rescue Nora.

Who, he reminded himself, had not wanted to be rescued before. He hoped *she* didn't start shooting at him too.

He sent the dun zigzagging down the slope toward the camp and threw a shot at Wallace as he did so. The bandit chief fired again, and Longarm felt the dun suddenly stagger. Long years of experience told him that the horse was going down. He kicked his feet free of the stirrups and threw himself out of the saddle as the dun fell and tumbled down the side of the sand hill.

Longarm did some tumbling himself. He tried to keep his gun out of the sand, not wanting the barrel to be fouled. Another bullet from Wallace's rifle kicked up grit that got into his eyes. Longarm blinked furiously to clear his vision as he came back up on his feet. He saw to his surprise that the dun was up as well. He had thought the horse was mortally wounded. Instead, Longarm saw only a long red crease on the animal's flank. The wound had been bad enough to make the horse stumble and fall, but not fatal.

Far from fatal, in fact. The dun put its ears back and galloped straight at Wallace. The outlaw had to leap aside desperately to avoid being trampled.

Longarm was ready by then. He took deliberate aim and squeezed off two shots. The range was still long, but the big lawman's aim was accurate. Both bullets slammed into Wallace's body and threw him backward onto the sand.

Longarm saw movement from the corner of his eye as he hurried toward Wallace's sprawled figure. Nora was running away. Wallace wasn't moving, so Longarm risked postponing checking the outlaw leader to make sure he was dead. Longarm changed direction to intercept Nora instead. Running through the soft sand was difficult for both of them, but Longarm's longer strides enabled him to catch up. He lunged forward, wrapped his left arm around Nora's waist, and bore her to the ground as he fell too.

"Hold it!" he said urgently to her. "Damn it, stop fighting! I know all about Palmer! I know he wants to kill you! Blast it, Miss Canady, I won't take you back to him!"

The words finally got through to her. She sagged back against the hot sand and peered up at Longarm. "You . . . you know about Jonas?" she gasped.

"Not all of it, but enough," he snapped. "Get it through your head, gal, I'm on your side."

"A-all right."

"Are you through fighting with me?"

She nodded. Longarm pushed himself to his feet and took her hand to lift her to hers. "Come on," he said. "We've got to get out of here while we've got the chance."

Hand in hand, they hurried toward Longarm's horse, which had stopped near the corral. Wallace's mount was still there. Longarm intended for Nora to use it, since Wallace no longer had any need for the animal. Wallace lay on his back, staring sightlessly up at the clear blue West Texas sky. His eyes were already turning glassy. He wouldn't be cooking any more meals.

"Can you ride bareback?" Longarm asked Nora.

She nodded. "I . . . I think so."

He hoped so, because that meant he wouldn't have to take the time to saddle Wallace's horse. He had become aware that there was an ominous silence coming from over the dune where the battle had taken place. That might mean that all the outlaws, as well as Carter and all of his men, were dead.

Or it might not.

Longarm helped Nora onto the horse, then ran to grab the dun's reins. He swung up into the saddle, then rode over to join her. "Let's go," he told her. "Just kick your feet against the horse's sides to get it moving, and hang on to the mane."

She looked scared as hell, and he didn't blame her. He was still a mite nervous himself. They rode south, hoping to skirt around anyone who might have been left from the shoot-out in the dunes. As he rode, Longarm thumbed fresh cartridges into the cylinder of the Colt.

They had only gone a couple of hundred yards when, with a slither of sand, a rider topped the hill to their right and fired a rifle at them. The bullet slammed into the sand a few feet in front of Longarm. He figured it was a miss on purpose, to force them to rein in. He did so as the rider came sliding down the slope, keeping them covered with a Spencer carbine.

It was Simeon Carter.

He and Nora had been mighty lucky so far, thought Longarm, but now it looked as if their luck had just run out.

Chapter 19

Carter kept the carbine trained on them as he rode down the slope toward them. Something about the way the man was sitting in the saddle struck Longarm as odd, and as Carter approached, Longarm saw a red stain spreading across the middle of his shirt. Carter was gutshot, which meant he was pretty much doomed. He wasn't going to survive this encounter.

But he was clearly determined that his intended targets weren't going to either.

Awkwardly, Carter reined in when he was about twenty feet from Longarm and Nora. He held the carbine in his right hand, the reins in his left. Even though he was badly wounded and was holding the carbine with only one hand, its barrel didn't waver. Hired killer or not, the gent had a hell of a lot of will, and Longarm could almost admire that.

"Might as well give it up, Carter," said Longarm. "You're not going to make it back to Monahans."

An ugly grin pulled Carter's lips back from his teeth. He wasn't the most attractive fellow in the world to start with, and now, with his face made gaunt and haggard from pain, he looked like hell. He laughed and said bluntly, "No, I won't make it back. But neither will you, Long. And as for the young lady . . ."

"You're going to kill her too."

"I took the senator's money." That summed it all up as far as Carter was concerned. He had been paid to do a job, and he would do it with his dying breath, if that was what it took.

Longarm took a stab at something. "You know, Palmer would have killed you too once you disposed of me and Miss Canady. He couldn't afford to let you live either."

"He might have tried," rasped Carter.

"Oh, he'd have found a way. He couldn't leave you alive to maybe testify someday that he had his own fiancée murdered. He would have been afraid too that you might try to blackmail him."

Carter looked offended. "He never would have even seen me again, once the job was done."

"Well, now he doesn't have to worry about it, does he? Because you're going to be dead, Carter. The senator wins, all the way around."

"Doesn't matter to me." Blood had pooled on Carter's saddle and was now dripping off it, falling with a steady *plop-plop* onto the ground, where it was rapidly sucked up by the ever-thirsty sand. "I'm gone either way." The hired killer lifted the barrel of the Spencer a little. "And so are y—"

He swayed in the saddle before he could finish the sentence, and that was what Longarm had been waiting for, the reason Longarm had stalled. Loss of blood had made Carter dizzy and almost made him fall. Longarm seized the chance.

His gun came up and bucked against his palm as he fired. The Spencer erupted at practically the same instant, but Longarm's shot came a fraction of a second quicker. The slug took Carter high on the chest and drove him backward out of the saddle. The carbine's barrel had already tipped up slightly when he squeezed the trigger, sending the bullet harmlessly over the heads of Longarm and Nora. Carter's body thudded loose-limbed onto the sand and didn't move again.

160

A faint whimpering sound came from Nora. She had to realize how close she had just come to dying.

But close didn't mean much in a corpse-and-cartridge session like this, Longarm thought as he heeled the dun over next to the fallen killer. He held the gun ready just in case as he dismounted and checked Carter's body. The man was dead, all right. And he had evidently been the only survivor of the earlier shootout. Nobody else had shown up, and the only sounds to be heard were the faint moan of the wind and the tiny rustling of the eternally shifting sand.

Longarm holstered his gun and turned the dun back toward Nora. She watched him with eyes made wide by fear and shock as he approached. "Is . . . is he dead?" she asked.

"As can be," said Longarm with a nod. "Now, we'd better make tracks for Monahans just in case there's anybody left alive out here besides us."

He hitched his horse into motion, and Nora fell in beside him. After a moment, she said, "You really won't make me go back to Jonas?"

"I reckon you'll be seeing the senator again sooner or later," Longarm said, "when he stands trial for everything he's done."

The shadow of a smile passed over Nora's face. "I'd like that," she said.

It was late afternoon when the two of them reached Monahans. During the long ride, Nora had confirmed for Longarm that none of the outlaws had harmed her.

"Some of them wanted to . . . to molest me, I think," she had said. "But Mr. Wallace made it clear to them that he would kill them if they touched me. And the one they called Dutchy, he was nice to me too. Mr. Van Horn kept looking at me, but he . . . he never did or said anything to hurt me."

"Wallace wanted that ransom," Longarm had pointed out to her.

"Yes, I know. Mr. Van Horn had written a letter to my father asking for money. He was going to take it into town

161

and mail it." She'd shaken her head. "He never got around to it."

Now, as they rode slowly down the main street of the settlement, Longarm saw a familiar face as a man stepped out onto the boardwalk from one of the stores. Walt Gibson, the middle-aged rancher who had been on the stagecoach when Nora was kidnapped, dropped the package he was carrying and shouted, "You son of a bitch!" as he reached for his gun.

Longarm had the Colt out of the cross-draw rig and leveled before Gibson could clear leather. "Don't do it, Walt," he warned the cattleman. "You don't know what happened out there."

Nora leaned forward anxiously. "That's right, Mr. Gibson," she said, remembering the man from the time they had spent together as passengers on the stagecoach. "Marshal Long rescued me from the bandits. He may have even saved my life."

Gibson looked dubious, and the crowd that was beginning to gather looked confused, but after a moment the rancher took his hand away from the butt of his gun. "You mean this fella's a lawman, Miss Cassidy?"

"Yes, he is." Nora glanced over at Longarm. "And it's Canady, Nora Canady." She flushed. "I'm sorry I had to use a false name earlier."

Clearly, her real name didn't mean anything to Gibson. He gave Longarm a grudging nod as Longarm holstered the Colt. "I reckon I'll take the young lady's word. I ain't forgot that clout you gave me, though, mister."

"And I'm right sorry about it too, Walt," said Longarm. "Seemed like the thing to do at the time."

Gibson snorted and bent to pick up the package he had dropped. "The lady looks like she could use somebody to look after her for a while. Come with me, ma'am. I'll see you over to the boardinghouse. Mrs. Rawlings will take good care of you."

Nora slid down from the horse with Gibson's assistance,

then said to him, "Do you . . . do you think I could get a bath?"

Gibson blushed a little. "We'll see about it, ma'am," he promised.

Before they could walk across the street to the boarding-house, Longarm asked Gibson, "Is there a regular lawman in this town?"

"Sheriff's away. But there's a troop of Rangers down at the Ace High."

That was the best news Longarm had heard in a long time. The Rangers could help him round up Jonas Palmer and Emily Toplin, and they could make sure as well that Nora remained safe. As he heeled the dun into a walk, he said to Gibson, "Keep an eye on the lady, Walt. There could still be trouble."

Grim-faced, the cattleman nodded.

Longarm found the Rangers sitting around a couple of tables in the Ace High Saloon, some of them engaged in a desultory game of poker. Their leader, a solemn young man who introduced himself as Lieutenant Gillette, shook Longarm's hand and nodded at the bloodstain on the marshal's side.

"Looks like you could use a sawbones," Gillette commented.

"I'll be all right. There's something else I need more right now, and that's somebody to back my play."

"Whatever you say, Marshal."

"Let's head down to the Sure Shot." Longarm figured that with a troop of Texas Rangers at his back, he could arrest even a United States senator.

The only problem with that idea was that Jonas Palmer was gone.

"He and the gal who was with him left this morning," explained a bartender who was obviously startled by the amount of firepower standing around in his saloon.

"You mean Miss Toplin?" asked Longarm.

The bartender nodded. "Yes, sir, that's her."

163

So Emily had either gotten loose, or somebody had come along and untied her. Either way, she had gotten back to Palmer, and both of them had lit a shuck out of Monahans as soon as possible. "How'd they leave?" Longarm asked.

"Caught the northbound stage."

That figured. Palmer wouldn't wait around to see if Carter caught up to Longarm or not. The senator was probably running back to Denver as hard as he could right about now. He would hope that Carter succeeded in killing both Longarm and Nora, but just in case of more trouble, Palmer would want to be back home, where he was in his strongest position.

Disappointed, Longarm went back to the Ace High with Lieutenant Gillette and the other Rangers. Over several shots of Maryland rye—lifesavers, every one of them, as far as Longarm was concerned—he explained everything that had happened during the past couple of weeks. Everything he knew, that is. There were still some questions that Nora was going to have to answer.

"We'll take a ride out into the sand hills first thing tomorrow morning," promised Gillette. "The bodies of those outlaws and Carter and his men will need to be brought in."

"Was that your ambush I ruined a few days ago?"

Gillette nodded. "We would have given Wallace and his bunch a chance to surrender if you hadn't come along and warned them." The Ranger gave Longarm a cool stare. "You're lucky things worked out as well as they did."

"I reckon you're right," Longarm agreed mildly. He tossed back what was left of the liquor in his glass.

Gillette gestured at one of his men. "My sergeant has quite a bit of experience in patching up bullet holes. Maybe he'd better take a look at you."

"Wouldn't hurt," said Longarm. He was suddenly extremely tired. He started to stand up. . . .

And promptly fell over onto the sawdust-littered floor, upsetting his chair and causing Gillette to exclaim in surprise.

Longarm had pushed his tired, battered body as far as he could, and now he was out cold.

At some point, Longarm woke up enough to realize that someone was helping him into a bed covered with soft, cool sheets. He murmured something, then dozed off again.

He had slept all night, he discovered when he awoke the next morning. The wound in his side had been cleaned again, and the bloodstained bandages around his midsection had been replaced. Fresh clothes lay on a chair, so he got up and got dressed, moving rather slowly so that sore and stiff muscles wouldn't protest too much. He guessed that he was in the boardinghouse; the room, with a rug on the floor and a crocheted bedspread and flowery wallpaper, looked like a boardinghouse room.

He was on the second floor of the building, he found when he stepped out into the hallway. A staircase led down to a foyer. Longarm descended the stairs carefully, hanging on to the banister.

Nora must have heard his footsteps, because she stepped into the foyer from one of the other rooms to wait for him. She was smiling broadly as she looked up the stairs at him. Her hair had been washed and hung in loose, luxurious waves down her back. She wore a light blue dress that matched her eyes.

"Good morning," she said. "I was about to decide you were going to sleep the day away."

"Well, you're a heap more chipper than you were the last time I saw you," Longarm said dryly.

"Mrs. Rawlings has taken good care of me, just like Mr. Gibson promised. And he's such a nice man too." She took Longarm's arm when he reached the bottom of the stairs, linking hers with it as she turned him toward what he now saw was a dining room. "And of course those Rangers have been very helpful, especially that handsome young Lieutenant Gillette."

Longarm frowned a little at the admiration in her voice.

Not that it mattered to him who she thought was handsome, he told himself.

"Who put me to bed yesterday?" he asked.

"That was Lieutenant Gillette, with the help of his sergeant." Nora laughed. "The Lieutenant said you called him Beth. Who's Beth, Marshal Long?"

Longarm felt himself flushing. "Just a friend."

"An old friend?"

"Not so old," said Longarm. He sniffed the air in the dining room. "Oh, Lord. Is that bacon I smell?"

"And eggs and hotcakes and fried potatoes. Here, sit down. I'll bring you a plate. I've made sure that Mrs. Rawlings kept some of the food warm for you."

The next half hour was a little bit of heaven for Longarm. He ate everything Nora placed in front of him, even though she had go to back to the kitchen three times. He put away a whole pot of coffee too, and when he was finally finished he leaned back in his chair and sighed. He reckoned he would live after all.

Nora was sitting on the other side of the table, watching him with amazement in her eyes. "I've never seen anyone eat like that," she said.

"You grew up around rich folks and politicians," Longarm said bluntly, "instead of people who work for a living."

Instantly, he regretted reminding her of her background. A shadow crossed her eyes, and the smile on her lips disappeared.

It was just as well, Longarm told himself. The last half hour had been mighty nice. . . .

But it was time for some answers, and he was sure they wouldn't be pretty ones.

Chapter 20

"None of it would have happened if I had just done what Jonas told me," Nora said as she sat at the table in the boardinghouse dining room with Longarm. Her hands were clasped together in front of her, and she kept looking down at the entwined fingers. "He said he just had to talk to my father for a few minutes, and then we could leave. We were going to the opera house, you see."

Longarm nodded. "Been there a few times myself."

"But I got impatient, and"—she stared down at her hands again—"and started to go back into my father's study to ask Jonas what was taking so long. The door was cracked open a bit, just enough for me to hear. . . ."

She swallowed hard and didn't go on. Longarm wanted to prod her, but instinct told him to take his time, to let her tell the story at her own pace.

"They were talking about the survey for a new railroad line my father is going to build," Nora finally continued. "The government is going to buy the land and then grant it to the railroad for a right-of-way. Jonas has seen to that. He's a committee chairman, you know."

Longarm just nodded.

"But the company that owns the land, the company that will make millions of dollars from the sale . . . it's not real.

167

It's actually just . . . Jonas and . . . and my father.''

"So your father's going to sell the land to the government, and then it'll turn right around and give it back to him?''

"That's right,'' Nora said with a nod.

"A pretty neat swindle,'' said Longarm.

"But that's not all of it. You see, the land's not really any good for a railroad. The grades are too steep, or something like that. I don't know much about such things, even though I grew up around them.''

Longarm's brow furrowed in puzzlement. "Then why go to all the trouble of selling it to Uncle Sam in the first place?''

"Because once it's discovered that the land is no good, Father and Jonas can get the government to provide more land for the right-of-way, land that *is* usable.''

Longarm mulled that over. "So he gets the land for his new railroad, plus all the money from selling the other land.''

"Yes. He and Jonas will split the profits.''

"But if the land that Palmer and your father secretly own won't work for a railroad, the survey should have shown that,'' Longarm pointed out.

"That's why they falsified the original survey, and they're going to make it look as if the surveyor, a man named Winston who has worked for my father for years, betrayed them and took money from a competitor to provide a false survey.''

Longarm took a deep breath and frowned again. "Dang it, when you put businessmen and politicians together, they come up with ways to steal money that are more twisted up than a skillet full of snakes. Why can't they just go out and rob banks like other crooks?''

Nora smiled sadly. "I couldn't believe they were ready to throw poor Mr. Winston to the wolves just so they could make more money. I've known him since I was a little girl.''

"So when you overheard all this . . .''

"I was upset, of course. I went away from the door of my father's study without them knowing that I was there. Jonas came out a few minutes later and took me to the opera house. I tried to pretend that nothing was wrong, but I suppose he could tell that something was bothering me. Later, he took me back to his house and . . . and persuaded me to tell him what it was.''

Longarm shook his head. "That was likely a mistake."

"He was furious. He said that I had to keep quiet, that I couldn't let my father know that I had overheard them talking. He said that I was going to be his wife and that I owed him my loyalty and my silence. He wanted me to promise . . . but I wouldn't. I told him I didn't know if . . . if I was even going to marry him.''

Again she paused, and again Longarm remained silent, sensing that what was to come was even more painful for Nora than the first part of the story had been.

Her voice lowered as she said, "When I wouldn't swear not to tell, he . . . he started tearing at my clothes. He said he was going to . . . to have carnal knowledge of me so that I . . . I would have to marry him. He said I would be ruined if I didn't. That way I would have to keep quiet.''

"That son of a bitch," Longarm grated.

"But I didn't let him. I fought back. I hit him—" Her voice dropped to a whisper. "Between the legs." In a more normal tone, she went on. "I ran out of there and managed to get home somehow. That night is such a blur now. But I knew I couldn't ever marry him. I was certain Father wouldn't allow me to call off the wedding, not when he had so much money riding on his deal with Jonas, so I decided to just . . . leave. As soon as I could, that's what I did.''

"How'd you get out of the house?"

Nora smiled. "Mr. O'Shaughnessy helped me. I've known him since I was a little girl too. He never could say no to me.''

So the big Irishman had been lying about not seeing anything the night Nora disappeared. That didn't come as a complete surprise to Longarm. He had already decided that she must have had help of some sort to get away.

169

"He even took me to the stage station and made sure I got aboard safely," she went on. "I know it bothered him terribly, because he felt as if he was being disloyal to my father, but he believed me when I told him how important it was that I leave Denver."

"You didn't tell him why?"

"No. I didn't want to put him in any danger. You see, I'd already realized that Jonas would kill me before he would allow me to ruin his plans. He told me as much when he was raging at me and trying to . . . to . . ."

Longarm reached over and patted her hand lightly. "That's all right. I know what you mean."

She shook her head. "He was like a . . . a different person. I couldn't believe it was him, that he would try to do such a thing to me. I . . . I'm a virgin."

Longarm didn't quite know what to say to that, so he just nodded and tried to look sympathetic. He had all the information he needed now. Nora's testimony would be enough to scuttle Palmer's scheme and save the government millions of dollars.

Assuming, of course, that she was willing to testify.

"If I take you back to Denver, will you tell your story to my boss?" he asked.

She hesitated, then said, "My father would be ruined."

"Maybe, maybe not. Back when folks were getting ready to build the transcontinental railroad, deals were made that were almost as shady as this one your father and Palmer are trying to pull. And your father's not the one who tried to have you killed. That was all Palmer's idea. I talked to your father twice, and all he wanted was to find you and get you back safely."

She caught hold of Longarm's hand and squeezed it. "I can't tell you how glad I am to hear you say that, Marshal Long. I . . . I suppose I can believe that my father is capable of stealing money—I heard that with my own ears. But to murder his own daughter . . ."

Longarm shook his head emphatically. "Not a chance in Hades, ma'am."

She smiled. "I can't allow Jonas to get away with it, can I?"

"Well, all I can tell you is that when a fella tries to kill me, I ain't usually in the mood to let him walk away afterward."

Nora's hand tightened on his. "I'll testify, Marshal," she said. "Get me back to Denver, and I'll tell the world what Jonas Palmer has done."

That was what Longarm wanted to hear.

And he hadn't even been forced to tell Nora about Palmer's mistress, which was good. The gal had been hurt enough already.

Lieutenant Gillette and the other Rangers rode back into Monahans that afternoon, leading the extra horses they had taken with them that morning. Bodies were tied onto the extra mounts, some of them carrying double. Longarm was sitting on a ladder-back chair on the boardwalk, talking to Walt Gibson, who was seated next to him. They saw the Rangers returning, and stepped out into the street to meet them.

"I reckon everybody's accounted for," Gillette told Longarm. "We found Wallace and all of his bunch, and Carter and all of his. All dead."

Longarm had already spotted Dutchy's body, and he felt a twinge of regret. He had almost liked the stocky outlaw. But Dutchy had known which side of the law he was riding on. Longarm couldn't feel too sorry for him.

He was glad, though, that Nora wasn't here to see the results of all the carnage in the sand hills. She was in her room over at the boardinghouse, and he hoped she stayed there until the Rangers got their grisly burdens down to the undertaker's.

Gillette hitched his horse into motion again. Longarm watched the Rangers ride slowly along the street, and knew that this part of the case was truly over. All that was left was getting Nora back to Denver and making her story public.

He walked over to the boardinghouse and went upstairs. Nora answered his knock and smiled when she saw it was him. "Hello, Marshal."

"Call me Custis," he said. "How do you feel about riding?"

She looked puzzled. "I don't know. I don't mind, I suppose."

"Good. I was thinking that instead of waiting for the stage we might ride over to Brownwood. Walt Gibson tells me there's a spur line there that runs up to Fort Worth, and we can connect with the Texas & Pacific there. We can get back to Denver a lot faster by rail, even if we have to go the long way around."

Nora nodded slowly and said, "All right."

Longarm could tell that something was bothering her. It was probably sinking in on her that she was about to go home to testify against her own father, as well as the man she had intended to marry. It wouldn't bother her to put Palmer behind bars, but despite what Longarm had told her earlier, they both knew there was a good chance Bryce Canady might go to jail too.

But then she took a deep breath and her chin lifted defiantly. "I'll be ready to ride whenever you are . . . Custis."

Longarm smiled. "Yes, ma'am."

The ride from Monahans to Brownwood, almost due east across the prairie and rolling plains of West Central Texas, took three days. Lieutenant Gillette and the rest of the Ranger troop accompanied Longarm and Nora, just to make certain there was no more trouble. The journey was peaceful, and within hours of arriving in Brownwood, the two of them were on a train rolling northeastward over the spur line toward Fort Worth.

Longarm smiled to himself as the train crossed a trestle over the Brazos River. A while back, he had paid a visit to the Brazos country and wound up chasing what was supposed to be some sort of monster. He had nearly gotten himself killed a time or two during that episode, and he wondered why he kept getting in such fracases every time he visited the Lone Star State. After all, he was a peaceable man, but folks kept trying to kill him anyway.

Time sort of ran together when a fella was traveling by rail, Longarm knew. From Fort Worth, he and Nora rode north to Kansas City, then changed trains and headed west toward Colorado. They spent hours talking, getting to know each other, and Longarm found the young woman to be mighty pleasant company. Nora was smart as a whip, even though her father had always figured her main asset was her beauty. She would marry an important man, such as Jonas Palmer, and spend the rest of her life as little more than a lovely adornment to him. That had been Bryce Canady's plan for her anyway.

A lot of things were going to change once she got back to Denver.

Nora and Longarm both had berths on the sleeper. Longarm had wired Billy Vail from Fort Worth to let him know that he was returning with Nora and that she was unharmed. Vail's immediate answer had been to spare no expense in getting the young woman back home. For once, Longarm's expense vouchers would not be questioned.

Longarm's wire had also warned Vail not to tell Canady and Palmer about Nora's return. Longarm was sure his boss was mighty puzzled about that, but he trusted Billy to honor the request.

Night was falling over the Kansas plains when Longarm and Nora left the train's dining car. Longarm was wearing a brown tweed suit he had bought in Kansas City. He tugged on the brim of his hat as he said to Nora, ''Well, good night again, I reckon.''

''Custis . . . don't leave.''

Longarm frowned slightly. ''Ma'am?''

''Don't call me ma'am,'' she said, ''and don't be so . . .

so thick. We're going to be in Denver by tomorrow night, aren't we?"

"More than likely," Longarm said with a nod.

"And after that nothing will ever be the same again."

He shrugged. "I reckon you could say that."

"Then this is our last night together, and I . . . I've made up my mind about something." She squared her shoulders and went on boldly. "I've decided I don't want to be a virgin anymore."

Her brazen declaration didn't come as a complete surprise to Longarm. He had sensed her growing interest in him. And as for him, well, she was a beautiful young woman and he was as human as the next fella, but . . .

"I don't mean any offense, Nora," he said quietly, "but I ain't in the habit of deflowering maidens."

"You've never been with a virgin before?" she challenged.

"Well, I can't rightly say that. . . ."

She stepped closer, and he could feel the heat coming from her. She put her hand on the back of his neck and came up on her toes to press her lips softly to his. The kiss started gently, almost chastely, but within seconds it had grown harder, more passionate and intense. Her body seemed to melt against his, her curves molding to him as his arms instinctively went around her.

She drew her mouth away from his and whispered, "I promise I won't weep and wail and carry on about my lost virtue. This is what I want, Custis. Really and truly."

Longarm was already hard, almost painfully so. When she reached down and rubbed the palm of her hand over the bulge at his groin, he had to bite back a groan of pleasure.

He began, "This is against my better judgment. . . ."

She smiled. "Then I'll just have to prove you wrong."

Chapter 21

She was as good as her word. There was no false coyness, no hesitation on her part when they were in her compartment. She undressed eagerly and openly, and she was just as eager to see Longarm's naked body. Her only moment of hesitation came when she saw the length and thickness of his shaft, and that slight nervousness was quickly replaced by anticipation as she wrapped her fingers around it. "It's rather . . . large, isn't it?"

Longarm managed not to laugh. He leaned forward instead and occupied himself with tonguing one of her erect pink nipples. Her breasts were fuller than he had thought they would be just by looking at her fully clothed. He cupped and molded them and sucked at the nipples until she was shivering with need.

"Oh," she said softly. "Oh, Custis . . ."

He eased her back on the bunk and parted her legs. The triangle of finespun hair that covered her mound was a shade darker than the honey-blond hair on her head. Longarm dipped a finger into her cleft and found her already wet and ready for him. He moved over her, positioning his hips between her wide spread thighs. The tip of his shaft found her opening and eased inside. She gasped at the sensation as her feminine folds parted to receive him.

He thrust forward slowly. There were two ways of doing this: fast and hard, so that the pain was over with quickly, or by taking his time so that she was thoroughly aroused and might not notice the discomfort as much when the moment came. He was going to proceed deliberately, he decided. He bent down to kiss her, and her lips parted under the stroking of his tongue. He eased his manhood more deeply within her as he reached down between them to tickle the little sentry just above the gate he had penetrated.

Nora started to squirm and buck under him, and she took her lips away from his to whisper urgently, "Now, Custis, oh, please, now!"

Well, if that was the way she wanted it . . .

Longarm drove his hips forward, feeling the fleeting resistance as the barrier met his shaft and then gave way. Nora might have screamed had her mouth not been pressed hard against his. Her bottom came up off the bunk to meet his thrust. Her hips pumped in time with his, falling into the age-old rhythm despite her inexperience.

The heat and the tightness of her sheath insured that Longarm's climax swept over him quickly. That was all right, he supposed, because by that time, Nora had already spasmed a couple of times herself. He drove himself as deeply into her as he could and held himself there as his fluid began to pour out in spurt after throbbing spurt. Nora clutched him tightly, her fingernails digging into his buttocks as he emptied his seed into her. Her head thrashed from side to side in ecstasy.

When Longarm stopped shuddering, he held himself up with his hands so that his weight wouldn't crush her and leaned down to kiss her. They were both breathless and covered with a fine sheen of sweat. Nora looked up at him and smiled. "You see," she said, "I told you I wouldn't cry."

But as Longarm looked down at her in the dim light of the sleeping compartment, he saw something shining in her eyes.

That was all right, he told himself. Right about now, he was feeling a little misty-eyed himself.

That was just the beginning. Nora had a lot to learn, and evidently she was determined to learn it all in one night. The lessons stretched on into the next day, and by the time evening was approaching again, there wasn't much about Nora Canady that could be regarded as virgin anymore, Longarm supposed. But she was happy about it, and if she was happy, so was he.

Unfortunately, evening wasn't the only thing that was approaching. The lights of Denver were already twinkling on the horizon.

Longarm and Nora left the train at the station and went straight to the Federal Building. Billy Vail knew when their train was supposed to arrive, and he was waiting at the office for them. He was alone, Henry having long since gone home for the day.

"Damn it, Custis—" Vail began, then stopped short and took a deep breath. "Begging your pardon, Miss Canady," he said to Nora. "I'm mighty glad to see that you're all right. You had a lot of folks mighty worried."

"I'm sorry, Marshal Vail," she said.

"When you hear her story, Billy, you'll understand why she left Denver like she did," said Longarm.

"I hope so." Vail looked at Nora. "But what I want to know is why this big galoot of a deputy practically ordered me not to say anything to your father and Senator Palmer about him finding you."

"It all ties in together, Billy," Longarm told him before Nora could say anything. He slid a cheroot from his vest pocket and went on. "We'd better all sit down. Miss Canady's got quite a story to tell."

Vail's eyes got wider and wider as Nora explained about the land swindle being planned by Bryce Canady and Jonas Palmer. His face flushed red with anger as he heard about Palmer's efforts to have Nora killed. When she was finished, he banged a fist on his desk and exclaimed, "Blast it, Palmer probably thinks he can get away with anything just because he's a senator! Well, he's about to find out different."

Longarm cocked his right ankle on his left knee and asked, "Do you know if he's in town, Billy?"

Vail nodded. "He's here, all right. Paying me a visit nearly every day wanting to know if I've heard anything from you. It wasn't easy lying to him the past couple of days, but now I'm glad I did. If he knew the two of you were on your way here, he'd have probably had somebody waiting for you at the station."

"Somebody with a gun," Longarm said dryly.

"How do you want to do this, Custis?"

Longarm leaned forward in his chair, glancing at Nora as he did so. She still seemed to be all right, a little pale but determined to go through with whatever was necessary.

"Send word to Palmer to meet us at Mr. Canady's house in an hour," said Longarm. "I reckon it's time for a showdown."

Jennings, the bald, solemn-faced butler showed Longarm and Vail into Bryce Canady's study later that evening. Canady and Jonas Palmer were both standing near Canady's desk, each of them holding a glass of brandy. Canady put his aside hurriedly and stepped forward to meet the two lawmen. His face was drawn tight with tension.

"Gentlemen," he said. He looked at Longarm. "I assume that since you've returned, Marshal Long, you have word of my daughter."

He thought Nora was dead, Longarm realized. He saw the grief in Canady's eyes, barely contained by the man's iron self-control. But it would have come pouring out if Canady had heard the bad news he was expecting to hear.

Longarm was glad he didn't have to deliver such news. There was that much to be thankful for in this mess anyway.

He glanced at Palmer. The senator looked tense too, but

it was a different sort of anxiety. For the most part, though, Palmer's stony expression was unreadable.

"Yes, sir," said Longarm with a nod. "I do have word of your daughter." He stepped over to the door Jennings had closed behind them and grasped the knob. "She's right here."

Canady gasped in surprise as Longarm threw the door open. Nora stepped through the doorway into the study, clad in a black dress and hat, with a veil over her face. She lifted her hands to the veil and raised it, and Canady cried out, practically sobbing with joy, as he saw his daughter's face. He took a step toward her.

A hell of a lot happened in a short time after that.

Longarm saw Palmer's right hand dive underneath his coat. The senator had to know that by now Nora had told her story to Longarm, Vail, and God only knows what other authorities. His career was ruined, and he faced years in prison, if not a hangman's rope. All that was left to him was vengeance—vengeance on the woman who had ruined his plans.

Longarm's Colt came out of its holster only a whisker of time after Palmer jerked a pocket pistol out of his coat. Vail yelled a warning and tackled Canady, knocking the railroad baron off his feet. Both of the middle-aged men sprawled on the expensive rug on the floor of the study. At the same instant, a huge form practically flew through the door, knocking Nora aside. O'Shaughnessy bellowed in rage as he threw himself toward Palmer. The gun in the senator's hand cracked once, and O'Shaughnessy stumbled under the impact of the bullet. Longarm fired an instant after Palmer.

The slug crashed into Palmer's right shoulder, shattering it and sending the gun flying from Palmer's suddenly nerveless fingers. Palmer screamed in pain and fell back on Canady's desk, his arm flopping loosely.

Longarm stepped over to him and kicked the gun away, then grabbed Palmer's shirtfront and jerked him upright.

"Quit your caterwauling, Senator," Longarm told him

through clenched teeth. "You'll live. Live to hang, more than likely."

Billy Vail was on his knees by now, looking down at Canady. "I hate to say this, Mr. Canady, but you're under arrest for trying to defraud the United States government."

Canady sat up. "So it's all come out, has it?" he asked heavily. He looked at his daughter, who was crying now. "Nora, you knew. . . ."

"I'm sorry, Father," she practically wailed.

Canady climbed to his feet. Under Vail's watchful eye, he stepped over to her and put his arms around her. "Don't worry," he told her, patting her back. "Are you all right? Were you hurt?"

Nora shook her head as she buried her face against his chest.

Canady smiled and hugged her. "Then that's all I care about. None of the rest of it matters. I've got my little girl back."

"No thanks to Palmer here," said Longarm. "He did his damnedest to have her killed, Canady."

The tycoon turned his head to look at his secret partner, the man who might have been his son-in-law. His lips drew back from his teeth. "I hope they put us in the same cell, Jonas," he said softly.

Judging from the sag-jawed expression on the senator's face, thought Longarm, Jonas Palmer had just found himself looking right into the pits of Hell.

Jennings was fussing over O'Shaughnessy, who was holding a hand over a bloody patch on his shoulder. "Oh, Lord, you're hurt, Fergus!" Jennings said.

"'Tis naught but a scratch," insisted O'Shaughnessy. "Ye did not think a wee gun like that could hurt me, did ye?"

"I'll summon a doctor," Jennings said before he rushed out of the room. Obviously, the hostility he had demonstrated toward the big Irishman during Longarm's previous visit to the Canady mansion was just a facade.

"Well, now," Billy Vail said as he looked around the room, "looks like it's all over."

Longarm looked at Canady, who was still holding his daughter as she cried against his chest. "Maybe," he said. "Maybe some of it's just starting."

The streets of Denver were quiet, and a hint of a cool breeze drifted down from the Front Range, relieving the warmth of the summer night. Longarm was walking because he felt like walking. He could have ridden in the wagon with Billy Vail and the two prisoners and the other deputies who were guarding them, but he hadn't felt like it. He probably could have stayed back at the Canady mansion for a while, where Nora was being looked after by Jennings and O'Shaughnessy and the other servants.

Instead he had felt the need to stretch his legs, to walk downtown and maybe get a drink, play a hand or two of cards.

Put this case and its tangled emotions behind him.

He drew deeply on the cheroot that was smoldering between his teeth. He and Nora had parted friends, and that was good. She had known that he and Vail were only doing their jobs. And she had whispered to him while they were momentarily alone that she didn't regret a thing they had done on the train, not a thing. But it would be a while before she would want to see much of him again, if ever, and he could understand that. He had to.

He wondered how Billy Vail would feel about giving him some time off, time enough to ride back down to Texas and see Beth Jellicoe again. . . .

The whisper of boot leather on pavement was all the warning he had.

Longarm spun around and spotted the figure lunging out of an alley mouth, heard the screamed curses, saw the gaping twin maws of a double-barreled shotgun pointing at him.

"Shit!" said Longarm.

He had forgotten all about Badger Bob McGurk.

He went diving for the ground as McGurk triggered both barrels of the Greener. The orange flare of the muzzle blasts lit up the night and cast the ugly features of the vengeful outlaw in a garish light. Longarm's gun was in his hand as he landed on his belly and felt buckshot sting his back as it grazed him. He fired twice, and both bullets caught Badger Bob in the face, making him even uglier as well as dead. McGurk flopped backward, dropping the scattergun.

Longarm stood up, dug out a lucifer with his left hand, and flicked it into life. The light from the match showed him Badger Bob's sprawled body. The outlaw would never hurt anybody again. Longarm dropped the lucifer and ground it out under his boot heel.

Somewhere in the distance, a whistle was blowing. One of the Denver policemen must have heard the shot and was summoning help before he came to investigate, thought Longarm.

He holstered his gun and sat down on the curb to wait. After a moment, he said, "Huh." He had just realized that he still didn't know if the fella called Ross, Badger Bob's old cell mate, had been hired to kill him by Senator Palmer, or if Ross had come after him as a favor to McGurk. He might never know, because McGurk and Ross were both dead and Palmer wasn't likely to ever admit to anything he didn't have to.

Not that it really mattered, Longarm told himself, because the people who had tried to kill him hadn't succeeded. He was alive, damn it, alive and kicking.

Longarm took another drag on the cheroot, which he hadn't dropped even while he was killing McGurk, and blew the smoke out in a perfect ring. Then he sat there next to the dead man and listened to the police whistles coming closer and watched the cool night breeze carry the smoke away.

Watch for

LONGARM AND THE CURSED CORPSE

246th novel in the exciting LONGARM series
from Jove

Coming in June!

JAKE LOGAN

TODAY'S HOTTEST ACTION WESTERN!